THE WITCH AND THE ENGLISHMAN

/ / / /

J.R. RAIN

THE WITCHES SERIES

Published by
Crop Circle Books
212 Third Crater, Moon

Printed in the United States of America.

ISBN-13: 978-1976053207
ISBN-10: 197605320X

Dedication
To Sandra, Harriet, Donna, Eve, Sandy, Chuck,
Elaine and Andrew. My crew. They help keep
the J.R. Rain train chugging.

1.

"Hi, this is Allison. Thank you for calling The Psychic Hotline. How can I help *you* see into the future?"

It was early evening and I was nearing the end of my shift. My "shift" being the time I was scheduled to be logged into the Hotline's computer system, via my laptop, on my comfy couch. Once I finished my shift and logged out, I could officially get dressed and start my day. Yes, I worked in my pajamas, and, yes, I worked from home. It's a good gig, but challenging—and sometimes *strange*—work.

"Yes, hello," said a very crisp and, if I wasn't mistaken, English accent. English and Australian accents tended to sound similar to my untrained ears. Then again, I was just a simple girl from Las Vegas.

Of course, *simple* might have gone out the window a few years ago when I'd met my first vampire—and before I had been told that I was a witch. A very powerful witch.

So weird, I thought, once again shaking my head over the insanity of it all. But to the Englishman on the other end of the line, I said, "What's your name?"

"Don't you already know?" he asked pleasantly enough. "I mean, you *are* psychic, right?"

I didn't take offense at the question. In fact, I was usually surprised when it *wasn't* asked. In this case, I sensed the good-natured ribbing behind it.

I said, "You bet your ass. But once I connect with you, I don't just stop with your name. *All* your secrets will be mine."

There was a pause, and then a light chuckle. "You're joking, right?"

"I say, why stop at a name?" I swung my stockinged feet to the polished wood floor and sat forward on the couch. The Englishman had my attention. And when someone had my attention... they *really* had my attention. I found myself logging into him easily enough. "The real question is, how much do you want me to know?"

He laughed sharply. "Now you're making me nervous. I suppose I had that coming. It was a rude question."

"A fair one," I said.

"Okay, now I like you, too," he said in his clipped accent.

"Now, *that* I could have predicted. So, how can I help you, Billy?"

He made a sound that might have been a gasp.

I laughed.

"Well, I'm gobsmacked," he said. "Obviously, my name came up on your computer screen."

"Obviously."

"Caller I.D. or something?"

"Or something," I said.

"My name didn't come up on your screen, did it?"

"No, it didn't."

"I see."

Except, of course, he didn't see. Not really. I knew this by the way his energy level had dropped... and by the way he'd mumbled those last two words. Mostly, of course, I knew by his body language.

Yes, his body language.

Little did Billy know that I was presently "in" his house with him. Although relatively new to the world of psychics—at least, *paid* psychics—I was highly gifted in "remote viewing." Yes, I could do exactly what the term implied: I could "see" from a distance. In my case, I could see the surroundings of those I tuned into. And, I could see *them*.

I was *very* in tune with Billy.

Presently, he sat in a wide-open living room, looking through a big sliding glass door that overlooked a sweeping back yard. Rising above the treetops, in the distance were some familiar tall buildings. I recognized the skyline. Santa Monica, if I wasn't mistaken.

I didn't know how remote viewing worked. It's weird and freaky, and it only seemed to get freakier by the minute. I got freakier by the minute, too, especially since I was best friends with a vampire.

Yes, with a vampire.

That had a lot to do with my growing psychic skills. *Long story.*

Anyway, one of the perks of being friends with a vampire—or, rather, allowing one to *feed* from me, but not *kill* me, of course—was that my own psychic abilities were amplified with each feeding.

Apparently, just being in close proximity to a vampire also increased my psychic abilities.

So weird.

Happily, Samantha Moon and I did a lot more than just hang out and watch *The Vampire Diaries,* which I had gotten her hooked on. At least once a week, I allowed her to feed from me. Often, right after we'd watched *The Vampire Diaries.* There was a strange synchronicity to that. More than once, I had caught her making a mental note or two while watching the show. Samantha Moon was still a relatively *new* vampire, as vampires went. And her "condition," as she called it, didn't come with a user's manual. So, while I watched the show—because I, and most of the rest of the viewers, had the world's biggest crush on Damon—Samantha made mental "how-to" notes about the vampire mystique.

Yes, our lives were that weird.

Mine was only getting weirder.

Apparently, my friendship with Samantha stretched back through the ages, along with another friend of ours named Millicent, now deceased... and presently haunting my apartment. Millicent, Samantha and I had once formed a "triad" of witches.

Powerful witches.

Except, in this life, Samantha had to go and get herself turned into a vampire, and Millicent had pretty much insisted on ousting Sam from our witchy clique. So now, the witch triad was missing one of us.

Millicent, the strongest of us, had purposely passed on well before us, so she could guide and coach us from the spirit world. An interesting concept, surely. Now my apartment here in Beverly Hills was haunted by a deceased witch... and an old friend.

So very, very weird.

Of course, I didn't know any of this until Millicent had appeared in my life... quite literally. I learned we were born with a clean slate, only to be filled with that which moved us, inspired and pushed us forward.

I never thought I might be a powerful witch. Or even a not-so-powerful witch. Yes, I had always been intrigued by Wicca and witchcraft, but not inordinately so. Mild curiosity only.

Now, Wicca was my life, as Millicent trained and coached me almost daily... coached me from beyond.

"I'm afraid to ask what else you know about me," said Billy, after a moment. He was standing now, having moved over to the big glass sliding door. I went over there, too, shifting my focus so that I saw what he saw: a wide expanse of back yard surrounded in a lot of dead ivy and high walls. The back yard looked like something mentioned in T.S. Eliot's *The Wasteland*: empty, dark, and dead.

"Then don't ask," I said.

"You know a lot more than you're telling, don't you?" He held the phone loosely against his ear. He smiled, having pushed past the weirdness of the situation.

"Maybe a little more," I said.

"I wasn't expecting a phone call like this."

"I don't suppose you were."

"What else might you know about me?" he asked.

"Are you sure you want to know?"

"Yes. I think." He laughed lightly at that, but I sensed his growing discomfort. He shrugged and rolled his head around. Classic manliness.

I said, "Okay. Here goes... you're standing in your living room, looking out your sliding glass door."

He didn't move or speak for perhaps twenty seconds. Then he did what most people did when I laid the "I-can-see-you" card on the table. He turned and looked over his shoulder and, for good measure, he shuddered.

"You can see me now?" he asked.

"Yes."

"So, you really are psychic?"

"As psychic as they come... and then some."

"What am I doing now?"

"You're waving at me. Now you're pinching your nose."

"Holy sweet mother of God."

"Welcome to my life," I said.

"And welcome to my life." He winked at me.

"So, how can I help you?"

"I have questions about my daughter."

"What kind of questions?"

"I think..." he paused, started again, and I knew immediately he was withholding information from me. "I think she might be in a spot of trouble."

"A 'spot' of trouble? What kind of trouble?"

"Is this being recorded?"

"Yes."

"Is there any chance we could meet, say, in person? That is, of course, if you are local."

"It's against company policy. And, I'm not that far from you."

"So, you'll meet me?"

"Yes," I said.

"Where?"

"Your house."

"Do you need the address?"

"No," I said.

"I thought you might say that."

"Maybe I'm not the only psychic one. See you in a few."

I disconnected the call, but not before I got one last psychic hit.

And it was a big one.

2.

Yes, I could get fired over this.

No, I didn't give a shit if they fired me over this, although I would miss the steady paycheck and the interesting characters.

Millicent thought, however, that I should start my own practice, where clients came in to see me. I reminded her that she was just a ghost and what did she know, although that didn't sit very well with her.

Now, as I dashed through my apartment, slipping on my Asics and light jacket, the partial outline of a thirty-something woman appeared in my kitchen. I hadn't quite gotten used to Millicent's sudden appearances, and I was certainly not used to the way the hair at the back of my neck stood on end, as it did now.

As usual, she watched me quietly, hands folded before her, wearing the kind of dress my grandmother might have worn decades ago. Her outfit made sense, since Millicent had been my grandmother's age when she had died. Her face seemed younger, though, of late.

"You saw?" she asked. When Millicent spoke, sometimes her lips moved, sometimes they didn't. Either way, her words appeared directly in my head, just behind my inner ear. Same with Samantha Moon, that was, when we decided to communicate telepathically. It sounded weirder than it actually was.

"I saw," I said. I was looking for my keys. They weren't on the hook where they belonged, and that irked me to no end. Sure, I could telepathically fly around the houses of other people, remote viewing the hell out of them, but I couldn't find my own damn keys.

"They're in the bathroom. You were in a rush this morning, remember?" Millicent said.

"Oh, yes." Just like every morning, I had been rushing to the local Coffee Bean to get my decaf sugar-free mocha and rushing to get back. Yes, decaf... *and* sugar-free.

Sadly, caffeine and sugar hampered my psychic sensitivity.

Yes, it was a bummer, but I had convinced myself that sugar-free mocha tasted just as good, and just getting out of my apartment was a nice way to start the morning. Of course, getting back to my apartment on time, before my shift started, was always a challenge. Hence, the mad dash to the bathroom where I had left the keys.

I grabbed them and crossed back through the living room, heading for the front door. Millicent watched me calmly from my kitchen. Then again, everything she did was calm. No, she wasn't quite a ghost. She was a spirit. There was a difference, apparently. Ghosts were bound to a location. Millicent? Not so much. As a spirit, she could come and go as she pleased. And she pleased to come and go often enough. Not to mention, she could appear and reappear anywhere else, too.

"He's going to die, Allison," said Millicent as I approached the front door.

I paused and took in a lot of air. Without turning, I said, "I know."

"Allison?"

I continued not looking at her, although I sensed her approaching me from behind, sliding up next to me. I knew this because the hair on my neck and arms and most of my scalp were all standing on end.

"Yes?"

"You can't help him."

"Who said I was going to help him?"

"I know you, child. Perhaps better than most."

"That, and you have direct access to my thoughts."

I couldn't recall Millicent's personality in our

past lives. But in *this* life—or, rather, in her current spiritual state—she was as serious as hell. Then again, maybe that was the nature of spirits: a complete lack of humor.

"Not a complete lack, Allison, but I didn't come here to joke or humor you. I came here to educate you. To train you. To remind you of who you really are."

She appeared before me, blocking my path to the front door. I gasped at the sudden sight of her, denser and more defined. One would think I was used to the woman—or spirit—appearing and disappearing . But not yet. Maybe someday. And, yes, it was as if a fully formed woman stood in front of me. Correction: not quite fully formed. She was missing her feet and most of her hands.

So weird.

I held my chest. "And half the time, you scare the crap out of me."

Millicent didn't like it when I used words like "crap" or "hell," let alone, the bigger, more colorful words. This, I suspected, was a holdover from her previous, and slightly more prudish, incarnation. She frowned in mild distaste.

"I don't mean to scare you, Allison."

"I know, I know, it's just a lucky bonus."

She moved in closer and I could feel her warmth, an odd thing to say about a discarnate entity. Still, when Millicent was particularly energized—and excited—she veritably radiated heat. Granted, it was *my* heat coming back at me; meaning, she drew energy from me—and the surrounding household—which was why my lights flickered and my refrigerator hummed and sputtered.

She ignored my last comment. Millicent often ignored my jibes and jabs and witticisms. Instead, she said, "Part of your education, child, is to know when to step aside... and when to take action."

"And let nature take its course?"

She nodded. Now she was directly in front of me, so close I could see her irises. They might have flared briefly with a small fire... or that could have been my imagination. Had she had bad breath, I would have known. She didn't.

Once again, I soaked her in, studying her every feature, and as I did, I had brief flashes—as I often had when she was nearby, and especially when she made a full physical appearance, as she was doing now—of us as teenagers, in a long-ago time, in a forgotten forest, practicing our witchcraft... and loving every minute of it. There was, of course, another witch with us. Samantha Moon. The three of us were something to behold... and something to respect and to even fear.

Most of what I had learned in those bygone, forgotten days was lost to me. Sort of. With Millicent's guidance, I was quickly coming into my own, growing more powerful and knowledgeable.

Samantha Moon? Not so much. My undead friend was on her own path; that was, she was on the path of the bloodsuckers, which made the witch threesome a twosome. According to Millicent, we were stronger as three. Anything done in threes was powerful. From prayers to witchcraft.

Of course, I was presently the only mortal among the three of us, which was a problem. Millicent was still technically a witch, although a dead one. As I'd discovered, her being dead didn't matter much. She did naturally and easily on the "other side" what I was having trouble doing on "this side." Still, there were rules in place, rules that limited her involvement in this world—the physical world. She was a force to be reckoned with... and a witch, through and through.

The same couldn't be said for my friend, Sam. From what I had gathered, the witchy spark left her the moment she became something else. Or, more accurately, the moment something very dark and evil entered into her. It was something Sam was fighting to this day.

But that's another story.

The story I found myself in was troubling... but one that I was determined to do something about.

"No, child," said Millicent, who still used her manner of speech from her last incarnation. "Now is the time to step aside. There is great danger in that home."

"What kind of danger?"

"There is a presence, something hidden."

"Fine. Whatever. It can just stay hidden. But I'll be damned if I'll just let a man die. I can't do that."

"His death has nothing to do with you, Allison. His death is between him... and forces much greater than you and I."

I stepped around her, mostly out of respect, although I knew I could have just as easily stepped *through* her, too. However, doing so would've left me shivering for several minutes.

At the door, I turned back to her and said, "Well, this greater force is just going to have to back off."

"Allison—"

But I was already out the door.

3.

I was driving.

Traffic from Beverly Hills to Santa Monica always gets dicey the closer you get to the 405 Freeway. Luckily, I knew all the shortcuts... and yeah, I might have even used a touch of prescience to find the fastest route. Either way, I soon found myself on Wilshire Boulevard, where I passed many beautiful glass buildings that reflected the setting sun. I also passed smaller businesses that reflected, if anything, the proverbial American Dream. There were costume shops and gaming shops and tobacco shops and coffee shops and Irish bars and gay bars and Greek cafés.

When I passed the fourth Starbucks, I finally took notice and pulled into the drive-thru. I ordered a decaf latte with half and half only, secretly longing for a mocha, but knowing I was going to need all the psychic help I could get in a manner of minutes. So, no caffeine, dammit.

Now sipping contently, I headed back out into the heavy traffic and put my mind on what I had seen during my initial scan of Billy Turner. Yes, I knew his last name, too. I could have told him that, but I didn't want to freak him out too much. Besides, I was already freaked enough for the two of us.

After all, I had seen, quite literally, his death.

If what I had seen was correct—and thanks to Millicent, I had little doubt—it was going to happen soon.

In a matter of days, in fact.

I considered calling Samantha Moon, but I knew she would be with her kids, probably making them a dinner she couldn't eat. I also considered calling my other good friend, Bernice, a psychic of a very different type—that is, the not-so-very-talented-type —but she was working the evening shift at The Psychic Hotline. Yes, not all psychics at the Hotline were cut from the same cloth. My experience was that many were shams, although some had a *hint* of real ability, like my friend, Bernice.

For now, though, I figured I needed more information. That meant I needed to talk to Billy directly, and in person. There was still a small chance I had not read Billy correctly, which I doubted. I had to quell that doubt, another reason why I agreed to meet him face-to-face. His also being cute had *almost* nothing to do with it.

Almost.

I glanced at the address I had written down. Unbeknownst to Billy Turner, I remained psychically connected to him after the phone call disconnected. Once I made a connection with someone, I could stay connected with them as long as I wanted. In this case, I passed in and around his house, noting the house number and street address. *Yes, I'm kind of like a superhero.*

Perhaps most disconcerting was the darkness I'd felt in the house, the darkness that Millicent had alluded to. A real darkness, too. Bad things had happened there at one time in the house's past, of that much I was sure. What those bad things were, remained to be seen.

Soon, I turned onto his street, which was lined with big homes, big trees, and wide patches of bright green lawns.

A wonderful place to live, I thought. *Or die.*

4.

Billy immediately answered the door, looking a bit embarrassed and surprised to see me.

"I'm Allison."

"I can't believe you're really here," he said.

"I could pinch you," I said, "if that would help."

"Maybe later—wait, sorry, that sounded creepy. It's just that..."

"What?" I asked, as I stepped into the big home.

"Well, I hadn't expected you to be so, well, lovely."

"Hearing you say that in your cute English accent makes me almost believe it."

He smiled at that, and as he did so, I saw again what I had seen earlier: the black aura that surrounded him. I could see auras around most people.

In fact, I could see them around just about everyone. Auras were an interesting thing, and I was only just beginning to learn about them. From what I now gathered, thanks to my many conversations with Samantha and Millicent, auras were an extension of our spiritual bodies. Most were interlaced with color. The colors often indicated someone's mood or intention. I was learning to understand what the colors meant.

There was, of course, no mistaking the meaning of the color black. Samantha had told me the story of her son, Anthony. She had seen the black aura around her son—and had known he would die unless she did something about it. Well, she had done something—something big—and it had changed the course of his life, perhaps forever.

She, too, had been warned not to mess with her son's fate... but she had done so anyway. It had been a decision that most people would respect, I believed. I certainly did.

But, like with all decisions, there were consequences—and now her son wasn't like other boys his age. Not quite a vampire, he was something else. Exactly what, remained to be seen.

Now, as I brushed past Billy, some of the black residue that clung to his aura attached itself to me, and broke free. I gasped a little and waved it away, where it disappeared in a puff. But before it did, I saw an image that I wouldn't soon forget.

"Everything okay?" he asked pleasantly enough. "You look like you just saw a ghost."

Too startled for even a halfway witty response, I merely shook my head and headed deeper into the house. Except I didn't find solace in the big, brooding structure. In fact, I received just the opposite impression: a sense of gloom and foreboding.

I had known Billy was going to die... but I hadn't known how.

Until now.

Sweet Jesus.

He said, "I would ask you if you wanted something to drink, but I see that you beat me to it." He motioned to the iced coffee I was holding. I had forgotten I held it, and now it collected condensation and began to drip. I told him I was fine and asked if he had a trash can. He looked at the mostly full cup and shrugged. After seeing what I had seen, I had lost my appetite... and apparently, my thirst, too.

He threw out the plastic cup for me—yes, I knew it was coffee abuse. He disappeared for a moment, in the kitchen, I presumed, and then reappeared. He showed me over to his couch, where we each sat on one end.

The house had a familiar feel.

It was, of course, exactly as I had seen it just a while earlier. If anything, though, it was far bigger than what I had been prepared for. Bigger and darker.

"Nice place," I said.

He shrugged. "Most people find it kind of creepy. My daughter does."

"How old is your daughter?"

"Twenty-four."

"And where is she now?"

"In jail."

I'd been so focused on him and his bleak house that I'd forgotten the reason for his call. *His daughter.*

"Why does your daughter think the house is creepy?"

He shrugged. "Apparently, it has a history of creepiness. I guess in the Seventies, a few bodies turned up in the basement. And before that, in the Twenties and Forties, two different owners were charged with murder. I think one of the owners, in the Eighties, died in an insane asylum."

"So, what made you want to buy the place?"

He laughed, or tried to. "I don't believe in any of that stuff."

"Yet, you called a psychic."

"Well, I didn't believe in any of that, at the time."

"What do you believe now?"

He shrugged, looked around the living room, looked up into the dark, vaulted ceiling. As he did so, his black aura swirled and churned. "I don't know what to believe. My daughter, as soon as we moved in here, well... she claimed to hear voices."

"What kind of voices?"

"Not nice voices."

"Evil voices?" I asked.

"I guess you could say that. They told her to

commit crimes, to hurt people, and even to hurt me."

"Why didn't you move?" I asked.

"I didn't believe her. I thought she was just being cheeky and wanted to go back home."

"To England?"

He nodded. "Glastonbury."

"Why did you move out here to Southern California?"

"I'm a director."

"Movies?"

"Yes. Short films, mostly. I was nominated for an Academy a few years ago."

"Congratulations," I said, noting my voice might have trailed off. The reason it trailed off was because I had just seen a very dark shape materialize in the hallway... and then disappear again.

Very dark, very tall, and very inhuman.

Red eyes, too.

I did not just see that.

"You all right?" he asked. "My word, you just turned pale. I mean, all the color just drained from your face."

I decided to be blunt. In fact, I couldn't help but be blunt. In double fact, I wasn't even entirely sure what I side next, so startled was I, and, quite frankly, terrified, by what I had just seen.

"I think your house is haunted, Billy. Very, very haunted."

He laughed immediately, and, if you ask me, a little too sharply and quickly. "Blimey! Why would you say such a thing?"

"I saw something in your hallway."

He laughed again... and leaned over and looked down his hallway. "I don't see anything." He looked right at me, his face only a few feet from mine. As he did so, a shadow appeared around him... and his eyes flared red. "Maybe it's a figment of your imagination."

Except, of course, the voice didn't sound like Billy's. It sounded deeper, guttural... and evil.

Billy blinked, looked at me awkwardly, and sat back on his side of the couch. "What were you saying?" he asked.

Billy, I was certain, had just been possessed by the very thing I had seen in his hallway.

Sweet Jesus.

5.

I took in a lot of air, and wondered what the hell I had just stepped into.

A living nightmare. Complete with devils and haunting and possession and murder and death.

"You're sure you're all right?" he asked.

I nodded weakly. As Billy looked at me, the blackness within his aura swirled and shifted and spread over the couch like an oil spill, oozing slowly away from him, over the cushions and down through the cracks and seams. This was different than the entity that momentarily possessed him. This was his aura... revealing again Billy didn't have long to live.

"Are you sure you're okay?"

"Yes," I said, averting my eyes, and taking a

few deep breaths. "I'm fine, really."

"It's about my daughter, isn't it?" The fear and alarm in his voice unmistakable. He sat forward, elbows on knees, and literally wrung his hands. As he did so, the black mass that surrounded him sat forward, too... and wove in and out of his fingers.

Sweet Jesus.

I shook my head. "No, I haven't picked up anything yet about your daughter... I'm concerned by what I saw in your home. You haven't seen anything strange?"

He waved off the question. "Me? No. Not really."

"What have you seen?"

He looked highly uncomfortable. He adjusted the drape of his pants, shifted on the couch, cracked his neck. "Keep in mind, I've lived here for nearly two years, and haven't seen anything."

"Until?"

"Until just a few days ago."

"You live here alone with your daughter?"

"Now I do. I'm alone while she's in jail."

"We'll get to that," I said. "First, tell me what you saw."

"I haven't seen anything. But I heard... laughing, followed by weeping."

"Is that why you called me?" I asked.

He looked at me, studied me closely, and then looked away. His pale face nearly glowed in the half-light of the room. A single lamp, in the far corner, was the only source of light.

He nodded. "I guess I want to know if there is something in the house. But I think you have answered that question."

I nodded. "Why is your daughter in jail?"

He went on, "My daughter is accused of killing a shopkeeper. A jewelry store owner, in fact."

I nodded. I had heard about the crime, which occurred about three weeks ago. Not far from here. I waited.

He studied me some more, then said, "My daughter—Liz—told me over and over that the voice wanted her to kill. That it loved death. It loved blood."

"Jesus," I said. "And you ignored her?"

"What would you do? What would anyone do?"

"Have someone talk to her. Someone like me."

"Well, I didn't. I didn't know what to do. I've never believed in ghosts or hauntings or any of that stuff. I thought Liz was going through a phase... a phase that would go away."

"And now she's accused of murder," I said.

He buried his face in his hands and suddenly wept loudly. "Please help me. I don't know what's happening... and I think... I think there's a very real possibility that I might be going mad."

6.

It was later.

I was in my Accord, parked illegally along busy Robertson Street in Beverly Hills. Yes, the words "Accord" and "Beverly Hills" don't generally go together, and, yeah, I'm a bit of a fish-out-of-water type.

I'm not wealthy. In fact, I worked two jobs to get by. Tomorrow morning, in fact, I would meet with a new client: a young actress who had been in the movie *Marley & Me*. I'd have to Google her later to see who, exactly, she was. Truth was, I didn't care either way. Rich or not, she was a paying client, and that's all that mattered. Then again, if you lived in these parts, you saw actors and actresses all the time. And TV anchormen. And reality stars. And famous artists and musicians and everyone in between. Last week, I'd watched Charlie Sheen get shit-faced at a bar near my home. And it wasn't the first time I watched him get shit-faced, either.

Or even the second.

Oh, Charlie.

Now, as I sat in my Accord, as a seeming armada of oversized, shiny SUVs roared by, I knew I needed someone to talk to.

I checked the time on my cell. Samantha's kids would be settled in now, perhaps watching TV or playing video games. Samantha was probably in her home office, making notes in files on her next case. Or not. Maybe she was playing video games with them. She was close to her kids, which I admired. And she seemed to only be getting closer to them every day, which was also a byproduct of her vampirism; meaning, her supernatural gifts rubbed off on them, too. She especially influenced her daughter, who was quickly maturing into one hell of a psychic herself.

Samantha picked up on the fourth ring. "Hello, Allie."

I said, "So, now I'm a fourth-ring friend? One more and it goes to your voicemail."

"That you know how many rings before the call goes to my voicemail is a little creepy."

"Says the vampire."

"Tsk, tsk," said Samantha. "Not over the phone."

"Because Big Brother might be listening?"

"Exactly."

"And why would they care about us, Sam?"

"Because we're awesome?"

"I suppose so. I guess they could always capture you and use your blood to create a super army of the undead."

"Are you quite done with this topic?" asked Sam.

"Yeah, sorry," I said. "I've had a tough day."

She paused, and I felt Sam scanning my thoughts. Yes, she and I were connected telepathically, even over long distances. Her feeding on me had a lot to do with that. Anyway, it's sometimes easier just to have her scan my thoughts, rather than relay them verbally. Telepathic communication was, if anything, efficient.

"Ah," said Sam when she was done. The scan only took seconds. Telepathic communication was fast, too. Everyone should try it.

"'Ah' is right," I said glumly. I had pulled over to the side of the road, not to admire the passing autocade of the world's nicest cars, but because I was still too shaken to drive straight. And... I couldn't think of anywhere to go. I just needed to stop and think and cry and talk.

"You've had quite a day," said Sam. Her voice was soothing and full of the kind of understanding that only two people who are deeply connected could have. After all, she had literally just relived the highlights—and lowlights—of my day.

"Sometimes it sucks being me," I said.

"Join the club," said Sam, with a small laugh. "Then again, part of what you have become is because of me, so I'm sorry for that."

"Nah. Don't be sorry. I'm just having a pity party. Truth is, I wouldn't trade what I am now for anything in the world. And you didn't force me to hang around with you, unless you did some weird mind trick on me or something."

"I have a few tricks up my sleeve, but that's not one of them. And they call it 'compulsion' on *The Vampire Diaries*."

Hearing Sam make real-life comparisons to *The Vampire Diaries* was amusing and surreal all rolled into one. I said, "Well, you've compelled people to tell you the truth in the past."

"That was just a momentary, passing thing. I barely knew what I was doing."

I said, "So, you don't think you could compel people for longer periods of time?"

I could almost see Sam shrug on her end of the line. Correction, I *could* actually see her shrug. I had, after all, a minor visual image of her on the periphery of my thoughts. It was an almost automatic link-up to her, a link-up that just happened without my trying. Yes, she and I were deeply connected.

"I don't know, but I'll look into it."

"It's a good thing you're a good you-know-what, Sam."

"For now," she said, in a rare instance of negativity. I knew Sam the vampire wasn't entirely sure how long she could remain "good," which, of course, was a relative term. The thing within her—a very dark entity that had gained access to this world through her—was doing its best to control her... and to possess her completely. Such dark entities were the driving force behind vampires and werewolves. Yes, werewolves. And, yes, I even knew of a werewolf. Hell, I might have even had a small crush on him, too. Except, of course, he was Samantha Moon's ex-boyfriend. Not to mention, he still carried a torch for her. *A major torch for her.* But, dammit, he was just so... yummy.

"Are you quite done?" she asked.

"Er, sorry."

"I mean, I can literally feel you lusting after Kingsley. That's kind of gross."

"Sorry. He's just so... never mind."

"Yes, he is yummy," said Samantha, reading my mind. "He's also a playboy and a cheat."

"He was set up, Sam. Some would make the argument that it wasn't even his fault."

"Some?" I heard the bite in her voice.

"Not me, of course," I said quickly. I didn't like pissing off my friend. Not to mention, it was probably never a good idea to piss off a vampire, especially a vampire who was presently battling a deeper darkness within. A darkness that could, at any moment, take total control of her. "But let it be known that I am officially on record for having an innocent crush on Kingsley."

"Fine, whatever. Now, can we change the subject? Like back to why you called me in the first place?"

I nodded, but the truth was, I was enjoying not thinking about Billy Turner's imminent death... or the thing that stalked his house. Outside my car, a couple were walking hand-in-hand. There had been an older photo of Billy and his daughter holding hands, too. Life could be so good in one moment... and so wrong the next.

"Billy Turner is going to be murdered, isn't he?" asked Samantha suddenly.

"Yes."

"But you don't know who kills him."

"No."

"I don't need to be a mind reader to know what you're thinking, Allie."

"Well, wouldn't you?" I asked.

She paused for only a nanosecond. "Yeah, I probably would do anything I could to save him, too."

"It seems like the obvious thing to do," I said.

"It does," said Sam.

"Except..."

"Except what?" asked Sam.

"Except Millicent thinks it's very much the *wrong* thing to do."

"Millicent is an old prude. Not to mention, she's dead. I'm not sure I like her."

"We were all friends once, Sam. In fact, we were friends in many, many lifetimes."

"Yeah, well, I don't know her in *this* lifetime. And, as far as I'm concerned, she's an old fuddy-duddy who's kind of creepy."

"She's more of a guide than a ghost, Sam. She knows what she's doing and she's teaching me to, you know, control what I am."

"Well, there's something about her that doesn't sit right with me. Something that bothers me."

I suspected I knew what that something was and gave Sam access to my suspicion.

"Maybe," said Sam.

"There's no maybe about it. She rejected you. In essence, she told you that you were not worthy to be the thing that we had been throughout many life-times. In effect, she cast you out of our little witch circle."

Sam said nothing. Her own husband had rejected her, too, and I knew that had scarred her, even to this day, and even though the man was quite dead.

"It doesn't mean she doesn't still like you, Sam. It just means you can't be, you know, a witch."

"Maybe I don't want to be a witch."

"You don't have to be a witch, Sam. You're something different. Something very special."

"Oh, bullshit. There's a she-devil living inside me just waiting to take me over for all eternity. But thanks for trying."

"Hey, I gave it my best shot."

Sam was silent, and so was I. My stomach, not so much. I needed some food... I also needed to know what I should do.

Sam picked up on my thought, as usual. "I say... skip all the psychic woo-woo shit, skip Millicent's advice, and get out of your own head. I say this: follow your heart."

"I like that," I said.

"So, what does your heart say, Allie?"

"It says to save him, no matter what."

"Then do that."

"And what if my heart is wrong?"

"We'll cross that bridge when we get to it."

"Except," I said, "I think I'm already halfway over it."

7.

"Hi, this is Allison. Thank you for calling the Psychic Hotline. How can I help *you* see into the future?"

"There you are," said a familiar voice.

I set aside my laptop and sat forward on the couch, elbows resting on my knees. "How long did it take you this time?"

"Fourth or fifth try."

"Less than before," I said.

"Things are looking up."

I grinned a little too big. Conn had that effect on me. As I grinned, and as Conn thought up the next witty thing he had to say, two things happened: one, I linked up to him; meaning, he and I were now deeply connected, although he didn't know it. The second, of course, was that I lit a cigarette. Yes, I smoked. No, I wasn't perfect. Yes, smoking helped calm my nerves. Hell, wouldn't you smoke if you were me, seeing the dead, and being friends with vampires and werewolves?

Not to mention, whenever Conn called... I just felt like lighting up. The way I liked to light up after sex. Of course, Conn and I had never had sex, or even phone sex... or had even met each other.

Months ago, he had called the Psychic Hotline, and we had hit it off in a way that startled me. Our connection had been immediate and strong, and he'd felt it, too. The mystery part was that I'd refused to see his face; yes, I could see him remotely, but I had refused to focus on his face. Well, all of his face. I'd stopped at his lips and jawline. That had been enough for me. Seeing too much of him just seemed like... cheating. Plus, I liked the idea he remained a mystery. Mysteries were good. One didn't always need immediate gratification.

Anyway, since then, he called me often, always waiting until he finally got patched through to me, often calling many dozens of times until he ended up with me. Then, we would talk for a long time... and rack up quite a bill in the process, since he was paying about $3.00 a minute. But, from what I had seen, he could more than afford a $3.00 a minute charge. But, until I met the man—*if* I met the man —he would remain a mystery. And Conn had been calling me now for, what, four or five months.

"Before I say anything, would you mind checking to see if we're alone?"

He did this often, which I appreciated. He was reminding me to double-check that we were alone on the line, as my bosses were sometimes tempted to listen in on us... and even record us for "training purposes," they claimed.

Of course, it was hard to sneak up on a psychic, and I always had a feel for when they were on the line, and so I told him to hold on and scanned the line. "We're alone," I reported.

"Good, so we can talk dirty?"

"We never talk dirty," I said. "And you had better be wearing pants, mister."

He laughed deeply at that. I knew, of course, that he was wearing clothing: shorts, in fact. He was sitting out on his upper deck—yes, he had lower deck, too—his preferred spot when he called me.

Conn mostly wore clothes when he called me. I said mostly because sometimes his clothing was no more than a partially closed robe. Today, he was wearing shorts and a tee-shirt, and he looked tan and healthy and full of life. An iced tea sat next to him. There was a mint leaf in the iced tea, and a slice of lemon. Yeah, he had it rough.

"So, when will we meet, Allison?"

"The answer to that is never."

"You sound so... firm. Is there any room for negotiation?"

"No," I said firmly.

"There you go again. But that's okay, Allison. I have you here with me now, and all is good in the world."

"You're a nut," I said.

He reached for his drink, sipped it, and sat back. I was tempted again to get a full view of his face. Was the rest of him as handsome as the lips and jaw promised? What did his eyes look like? It would be easy enough for me to see... all I had to do was focus...

But I refused to look. Not now. Perhaps, not ever. No, I would look, someday. But, for now, I liked this game we were playing.

"I want to meet you for dinner someday."

"That's not going to happen," I said.

"Aren't you curious to see me?"

He'd gotten me there, and I faltered before answering.

"There!" he said excitedly. "There's a chink in your armor. You do want to see what I look like."

"Fine. You got me. My interest is piqued, but it's not going to happen. Not in this life."

"So, you're saying there's a chance in the next life?"

I laughed at that.

"So, all I have to do is die and wait?"

"Now, don't get crazy on me," I said.

"I like you a lot," said Conn, "but not enough to kill myself."

"Hey, I think I'm offended," I said.

We were silent for a while. I was sitting forward, watching Conn in my mind's eye. Watching him from behind, to be exact, noting his wide shoulders and the way he loosely held his phone to his ear. I liked what I was seeing.

After a half minute, he said, "Is it possible to fall in love without actually meeting?"

"No," I said.

"I think," he said, "you might, for once, be wrong."

"Don't say it, Conn."

He didn't, but I felt it.

Dammit, I felt it.

8.

I had been a personal trainer before all this craziness.

I still did some personal training, which I enjoyed very much. The next morning, I met my new client, Ivy Tanner, who was even cuter than her IMDB pictures. I now remembered her from the movie, *Marley & Me*. She'd had a small role, but an important one.

We met at Gold's Gym in Beverly Hills, where I quickly assessed her strengths and weaknesses. She had a sore elbow from a fall off a horse while filming in South America with Russell Crowe not too long ago. She wasn't bragging. It was all very matter-of-fact. I nodded matter-of-factly as I put her through some lunges. I was so matter-of-fact that no one could have guessed that I had massive crush on Russell Crowe.

"Ah," she said, as she turned and looked at me, hands on hips, and lunging, "you are a fan of Russell Crowe, I see."

"That obvious?" I asked. I was lunging right alongside her.

"Well, your eyes lit up when I mentioned his name."

"I thought I was, you know, acting cool."

"You were acting, you know, cool... except for the fact that you looked a bit starstruck. Plus, I'm a bit of a psychic."

"Are you now?"

She nodded, sweat dripping from the tip of her nose. She might be beautiful as hell, but she was quite the sweater.

Welcome to the club.

"Yeah, I've been a little psychic my whole life. I'm always seeing things I shouldn't see, hearing things I shouldn't hear, and getting feelings that things are going to happen before they do."

I digested that, as we switched from lunges to squats. She wanted to keep the squats light, as she wrongly believed that squatting would make her ass big. I explained to her that they wouldn't but accommodated her request anyway. Besides, she had the bad elbow and I was okay with not putting too much stress on that.

As she positioned herself under the rack, with only a 25-pound plate on each side, I couldn't help but notice the many glances and outright stares directed our way. Or, rather, *her* way. Ivy, however, ignored them all. In fact, she could have just as easily been at home, working out in a private gym, for all that she noticed the looks and stares. I suspected not everyone knew her from her acting. She wasn't big enough yet. Still, she simply looked like someone famous. And in this town, that was sometimes good enough.

"I guess you think I'm pretty weird," she said, grunting a little as she squatted with almost perfect form. She was, I knew, twenty-four years old and, in today's fast-paced world of apps and widgets, that placed her nearly another generation behind me. Then again, I was only in my mid-thirties.

I said, "Even normal people are secretly weird."

She giggled and focused on her squats. When done, she slipped from under the bar as I repositioned it on the squat rack. She patted her face with a towel. "There are other things about me, too. Other weird things."

"Oh?" I said. I eased myself under the squat rack. After all, why not get in my own workout while she cooled down? Yes, I was basically paid to work out, and that tickled me to no end.

"I'm not sure why I'm telling you all of this," she said. "I don't normally go around telling people how weird I am."

"Don't worry about it," I said, waving it off. A young man literally stopped directly behind Ivy—stopped and gawked at her. I cranked out about triple what Ivy had just done. "After all, I might be just as weird."

"Really?"

"I'll tell you about it sometime."

"Okay, deal. So, do you wanna know what else is weird about me?"

"Boy, do I."

She giggled. "You're funny. Okay, now keep this between us, all right?"

"I'll do my best."

"I'm being serious, Allison. Something like this might, you know, hurt my chances in this town."

"With looks like yours, kiddo, I doubt it. But my lips are sealed."

"Oh my God, that was so sweet. Trust me, there are women who are tons prettier than me. Most of the time, I don't think I'm anywhere close to those other girls."

I wasn't sure if she was telling me the truth or telling me what she thought I wanted to hear. But as soon as that thought crossed my mind, I knew the answer was the former. The girl was oblivious to her own good looks.

I wasn't sure if this made me like her more or less. Either way, she was an easy-to-work-with client. Yeah, I liked her. A lot.

"Well, you're gorgeous, let's just settle that right now. And you're a fine actor, too. Actually, you're perfect and it's making me feel less confident about myself. Maybe we should get to the part about you being really, really weird, so that way I can start feeling a little better about myself."

She laughed. "You're funny, Allie. Can I call you Allie?"

"Sure, why not. You paid for ten sessions ahead of time, so you can call me whatever you want."

She laughed again, and then lowered her voice. "Okay, now this is going to sound really out there, you know? But... I think I might be a witch."

"Now, why doesn't that surprise me?" I said.

"Wait, what?"

"I think we need to talk," I said.

9.

"So, how long have you suspected you were a witch?" I asked.

We were both drinking unsweetened tea at The Coffee Bean on Third Street in Beverly Hills.

"Since I was a teenager, I've always been interested in anything and everything that had to do with witchcraft. I watched *Bewitched, Sabrina the Teenage Witch, Charmed, The Witches of Eastwick, Practical Magic*, you name it. I watched documentaries, studied Wicca. I thought it was normal to be interested in witchcraft. After all, there are women —and men—who are imbued with special powers. Women who look like you and me."

"Well, maybe like me," I said.

"Excuse me?"

"Never mind," I said. "I also have a job as a telephone psychic, but please, go on."

"Oh, you do?" She paused. "I mean, why wouldn't you be curious about Wicca? Why not look a little more into it?"

I played devil's advocate. "Well, many think that witchcraft is evil."

"Many are wrong. Wicca is an Earth-based religion. They are, if anything, more respectful to life on Planet Earth than many other so-called religions."

I didn't want to get into a heated discussion on religion and kept her on track. I said, "So you studied it."

"I did more than study it, Allie. I practiced it."

"Oh?"

"And what's more, I discovered I was damn good at it."

"Good at being a witch?"

"Right. I sort of had a knack for it."

"What does that mean, exactly?"

"It means that when I performed a spell... it generally worked."

I wasn't a "kitchen witch," which was a term generally applied to someone who used ingredients and such for their witchcraft. Traditional Wiccans often used various ingredients... and, no, not all that "eye of newt" crap. But real ingredients, some of which could be found in most kitchens. Turned out, I wasn't very good at that sort of stuff at all. The person who *had* been good at that was, yes,

Samantha Moon. She had, in fact, been the kitchen witch of our happy little trio in her former life.

I asked Ivy to explain more about the spells, and she said, "Easy ones at first. I did beauty spells. You see, I was never very pretty in high school. People used to make fun of me. Of my skin, in particular. I had very bad acne."

"You would never know it," I said, studying her, perhaps a little too closely. Dammit, I hoped I wasn't developing a woman-crush on her. "There are spells for acne?"

"Not necessarily, but you could always create your own."

"And you created your own spell?"

"It's easy, really."

"Sure it is," I said. "So, what else did you do?"

"Well, I wanted to be taller, too—"

The tea I had been sipping suddenly went down the wrong pipe. As I coughed, I managed to say, "You're kidding."

"No," she said, and gave me that sweet, dimply smile that was often featured on the posters of her many movies... the smile that directors loved to do close-ups on. "I grew three inches."

I was still coughing in spurts and fits. "Overnight?"

"No, silly. Growing spells don't work like that. Those take time."

"Of course they do," I said. "How silly of me."

The truth was, I didn't know much about spell-work. I would, in time, know more, as Millicent was adamant that I become a well-rounded witch. I now had a special cupboard filled with arcane, witchy ingredients. Millicent had overseen the collection of that, and my "spice" rack now boasted such oddities as mugwort and scullcaps and vervain. Yes, vervain, the very stuff that could weaken vampires. Shh, don't tell Sam. It was a real, witchy ingredient.

But, for now, my main studies had been centered on controlling the growing power within me—power amplified by my association with Samantha Moon.

Last night, Millicent had come to me in my dreams. And in my dreams, she had told me of a third witch. That was why I wasn't very surprised when Ivy told me that she was a witch. Was she the destined third of our little triad? It was looking like it.

As the late morning wore on, and as the pretty young actress told me more and more about her remarkable spellwork, I asked, "Have you ever performed spells to, you know, hurt someone?"

"Oh, no. Never." Then she blushed mightily. "Okay, maybe once."

"Tell me about it," I said. It was, I think, the first time in the history of this town that any actor blushed, ever.

"Well, I really liked this guy—"

"Uh-oh," I said.

She blushed some more. "Well, this was back in my first—and only—semester in college. He was a model and full of himself, but he was also kind of a bad boy, too. I mean, he rode a Harley to college."

"Nearly irresistible," I said.

"Tell me about it. Anyway, he had long hair, tattoos, and always knew just what to say. He especially knew how to..." She blushed deeper than ever.

"Turn you on?" I asked.

"Yes."

"Bad boys are good at that... but that's about all they're good for."

"Sounds like you've had your own experiences," said Ivy.

"Trust me," I said. "Every girl has had their own bad boy experience, and every girl will learn from them, too."

"Well, I learned plenty from Raul."

"Raul, huh? Very exotic."

"Yeah," she said, sighing a little. "Even his name did it for me."

"Oh, brother," I said. "Go on."

She told me the story. Raul had been a typical bad boy, saying all the right things, looking too cool for school, the works. Why he was in college was still a mystery until Ivy realized he was just there to pick up girls. Well, he'd picked her up, all right, and a few dates later, he'd really laid on the bad-boy charm, and the next thing Ivy knew, she'd found herself in his trailer—yes, trailer—wanting him more than any man she could ever remember wanting.

"He was my first," she said. She lowered her

gaze. Not in shame, but in sadness. "Wasted on that asshole."

"I'm sorry," I said.

Ivy glanced up at me, and her bright smile returned. "Trust me, it was all my fault. I've learned to take full responsibility for all my actions... and for all that I've attracted into my life."

I narrowed my eyes. "How old are you again?"

"Twenty-four."

"That's a seriously mature thing to have learned for a twenty-four-year-old."

"Well, I wasn't always like this. I had some lessons to learn first."

"Let me guess: Raul was the brunt of your lessons?"

She giggled, and continued: "We had sex that one time—one time—and the son-of-a-bitch disappears. And I mean, disappears. He won't return texts or phone calls. Nothing. I guess I was being a little needy, but, you know, he said all the right things: how much I meant to him, that he wouldn't hurt me, that he really liked me, that we had something special, blah, blah, blah. Then he fucks me and disappears."

I said, "Not all men are like that."

"I know, but I think Raul will seriously think again before de-virginizing another girl... and then splitting."

"Uh-oh," I said again.

"*Uh-oh* is right!"

"You seem, um, proud of what you did to him,

"No, not proud, but certainly not sorry."

"A woman scorned and all that?" I said.

"Exactly."

Although there was only one living person that I had a telepathic connection with—Samantha Moon—something interesting was happening with Ivy Tanner, something that finally got my attention: I could almost predict what she was going to say next.

Almost. Not quite.

"Okay," I said, "what did you do to the poor guy?"

"I shrunk his, you know, junk."

I looked at her. She looked at me. We stared at each other for a long, long time, and then, we both burst out laughing. That, of course, was exactly what I thought she was going to say.

"You shriveled his wiener?" I asked, gasping for breath.

"So small that he probably never used it again."

"Never?"

"Well, not unless he got very, very creative—and excited!"

"Holy shit," I said, wiping the tears from my eyes. "Remind me not to mess with you."

"Well, it's the only nasty thing I've ever done."

"Is it, um, reversible?"

"Oh, certainly."

"But you've never reversed it?"

"Oh, hell no. Not until he comes crawling back

to me with an apology."

"Does he know you're responsible?"

"Who the hell knows? I never heard from him again."

"Maybe he killed himself."

"No. Last I heard, he was partying harder than ever."

"And disappointing a lot of women," I said.

"One can only hope."

I shook my head and laughed some more. We both finished our teas and sat quietly for a moment.

"So," I said. "You really are a witch."

"I think so, yes. Does that surprise you?"

I looked at her some more, and as I did so, I raised my hands slowly. The table, which had been wobbling between us, quit wobbling... and *lifted* slowly off the ground. It continued to lift, the higher I raised my hands.

I didn't elevate it so high as to draw a lot of attention. Just enough to get Ivy's attention. And I had it. Completely.

Her mouth dropped open as she looked at me, then dipped her head under the table, then back up at me.

"Holy shit," she said.

I nodded and lowered my hands, and the table lowered with them, settling back into place, and still as wobbly as ever.

She said, "You're a... a..."

"A witch, too?" I offered.

"But... but, you're a personal trainer and, I think

you said, a telephone psychic. I don't understand all of this."

I smiled and said, "We have a lot to talk about."

10.

I was in my Spirit Chair.

Everyone needs a Spirit Chair. Or a Prayer Chair. Or a Meditation Chair. Whatever you want to call it. Stick it in the corner of your bedroom, living room, yoga room, basement, attic, garage... just wherever you can find some peace and quiet for about a half an hour.

My Spirit Chair was just an old recliner that was about as comfortable as comfortable gets, which was sometimes a problem. Sometimes, during deep meditations, I tended to nod off. Not a good thing.

Now, it was just after noon, and I had already showered after my session with Ivy... and after our long talk, too. I had a lot to process, including what to do about Billy's imminent death, his murderous daughter, and his haunted house.

In each hand, I held an object. In my right, an important stone to me, a stone I'd collected at Mount Shasta on a recent trip. It had been a trip where I had deeply connected with Mother Earth. In my left hand was a run-of-the-mill crystal that one could find in any New Age shop.

I loosely held both the rock and crystal, my hands in my lap. Legs crossed, comfortable in the Spirit Chair. Yes, it was also called a Lazy-Boy by those with less imagination.

Anyway, my head naturally lolled forward, my chin lightly pressing against my chest. I knew that the "proper" meditation technique was for my head to be straight. Screw proper, this was more comfortable.

More importantly, it worked.

At least, for me.

If nothing else, it was where I unwound, where I centered myself, and where I found peace in a very stressful world. In fact, right outside my bedroom window was the hustle and bustle of Beverly Hills where big deals were made every day, and spending a lot of money the norm. Out there, life was stressful.

In here, within my Spirit Chair, was pure bliss.

The crystal and rock were there for a reason, and not because I was into all that woo-woo New Age stuff, although a lot of that woo-woo New Age stuff was kind of fun, too. Whatever it took to connect to Spirit. My thing happened to be the

Spirit Chair and meditation. Someone else's thing might have been a prayer mat, a church, a walk in the woods, a yoga class, or watching *Late Night with Jimmy Fallon*.

Personally, I liked peace and quiet... and holding crystals. Crystals, for me, tended to raise my energy levels. Or, as Millicent called it, "raising my frequency," although I wasn't sure what she meant by that. All I knew was that crystals—and, in particular, the Mount Shasta rock—helped me to connect faster and deeper to the spiritual side of life.

That's what I was doing now.

I closed my eyes and held the stones loosely in my lap, wrapping my fingers around them just enough to have a good grip, but not so tightly that I wasn't relaxed. It was always a delicate balance to be relaxed enough to commune with the higher energies, but not so relaxed I found myself snoring softly. Or loudly.

Now, I was determined to stay awake, to truly connect to Spirit; or, in this case, one particular spirit.

A very big spirit.

Mother Earth, in fact.

There was, of course, no guarantee I would make the connection to her, although of late, she had taken an interest in me.

Yes, lucky me.

I took long, slow breaths, breathing in for two beats, and out for one beat. Always longer in than out. Drawing in the breath of life, as many traditions believed—and I thought, accurately—that our breathing connected us to the spirit world. Control of breath, control of thought, control of body... yes, that was the gateway into the unknown.

As always, I had done a small prayer of protection and guidance, letting my intentions be known. And my intentions were to contact peaceful spirits, loving spirits, and, if possible, Mother Earth herself.

In and out, in and out.

Stray thoughts appeared... my new witchy client, killers, blood and death, Russell Crowe's smile. I lingered on Russell Crowe's smile... then let that go, along with all the other stray thoughts.

I sought complete emptiness.

I sought complete release from this world, so that I could be untethered... and drift into the next.

Time passed. I wasn't sure how long went by. I didn't think it had been very long, but I had been wrong before. Sometimes when I thought only minutes had passed, whole hours, in fact, had passed.

Now, I was only vaguely aware of the passage of time. Mostly, I was aware that I'd slipped *out of time*. Yes, my body was sitting there on the Lazy Boy, experiencing time, but my mind had gone to a place both timeless and eternal.

It is peaceful here, although I am not sure where I am. It is peaceful and relaxing and I wonder if I am asleep.

Yet, I was aware of my body, of peace, of easy breathing. I was not snoring lightly, or even loudly. I was breathing easily.

Peace and eternity and timelessness... it was all here, wrapped in something beyond what I could comprehend, at least in my physical state. I was still too grounded to know, exactly, what was happening. But that was okay. I was not supposed to know all. That was the message I always received. Leave some mysteries for after Earth. Mysteries were a good thing. The mysterious compelled humans to search and expand and grow and evolve.

I felt another presence nearby, and from this presence emanated a great love... but not just for me... but for all of the world, *for* all of *her* world.

The amorphous shapes that had been swirling around me began to take shape, slowly at first, and then faster and faster, and then I found myself sitting on the crest of a massive mountain chain. One crest connected to another peak. On either side was a steep decline. One false step here, and one would fall seemingly forever.

Except, the mountain didn't quite feel real, or solid. In fact, I could see straight down through it, and down through the many strata of rock and sediment. Down there, I could see something glowing, pulsating, throbbing, alive. It was, I knew, the soul of the mountain itself.

No, I thought, it's *her*. It was *she* who was pulsating and vibrating and crackling everywhere, through rock, dirt, plants, the driest desert, or the richest soil.

She was everywhere.

For now, I continued sitting on the mountain.

Whether real or not, I didn't know, but the strong wind that buffeted me felt real enough. Few, I suspected, had seen this place, wherever I was. I was aware that there were many places on this Earth that were rarely experienced by humankind, and that was a good thing. The Earth needed a break from humankind.

I blinked... and discovered Mother Nature sitting directly across from me... legs crossed as mine were. She smiled at me.

"Good afternoon, Allison."

11.

A mountain goat watched us from nearby, chewing idly on some sparse grass that grew from under a cluster of boulders.

"It can see me?" I asked the woman sitting before me.

"Of course. Animals have no difficulty seeing into the higher realms. Their eyes are open. Only man is closed."

"But why?"

"It is as it should be. For now. But there will come a time when man can see further and deeper and higher. But now is not the time."

I had met her before, a few times now. She was Gaia, the spirit of the earth, the soul of the earth. She was Mother Earth, or Earth Mother, or the

Divine Mother. Each time I was with her, it felt like the first time. She had long, red hair, and long, white fingers, which were now interlaced on her lap. She wore a satiny robe that hugged her body and flapped as the wind blew.

"You choose this form for my benefit," I said.

"It makes it easier to relate to me."

"What would you look like otherwise?"

"My form is the mountain you sit upon, the earth you walk upon, the river you swim in, and the oceans you traverse."

"Why do you speak with me?"

The woman in front of me, whose hair lifted and fell, but not necessarily in conjunction with the blasts of cold air that hit us, tilted her head and looked at me sweetly. Correction: lovingly.

"Your question implies that it is a great privilege to speak to me."

"Is it not? You are Gaia. The earth spirit. You are our mother. You are so... important. I'm just me."

"Do you not feel special, child?"

I thought about that. "I do. But doesn't everyone?"

"Some more than others. Do not mistake great size, or great success, or great beauty, for importance. We are all equal in the eyes of the Creator, including me."

"But surely you are..." I couldn't say the words.

"More important than you?" she asked.

"Well, yes. You are home to billions of humans,

trillions of animal lives, to our history... and our future."

"But do you humans not create the history and the future?"

"I suppose so. But there are billions of us. You are one. You are a rock star," I said.

The woman before me smiled at my silly pun. Was I really sitting here on a mountain crest, at the back of beyond, joking with the spirit of the spinning rock which we called Planet Earth? I thought I was. Either that, or I was dreaming.

"We are all equal in the eyes of the Creator, Allison Lopez. We all have different jobs to do. Each job is as important as the next. Even the animals around you have their purposes."

"Surely, they are not more important than you."

"You are giving value again where no value exists; at least, there is none in the eyes of the Creator."

"Well, in my eyes, you are... awesome."

"And in my eyes, you are equally awesome."

I smiled at that... and was suddenly deeply touched. That Gaia, the spirit of our earth, even noticed me was almost too much to bear.

She reached out and took my hands. Her hands were so warm, so loving, so comforting.

"Why have you chosen to speak with me?" I asked.

"I speak to all my children. A few are ready for a deeper connection, as you are now."

"Why are they not ready? And why am I

ready?"

"Those who honor the earth move closer to me."

A long time later, after sitting quietly for many minutes or perhaps, hours, I opened my eyes and looked up, and again found myself in the Spirit Chair, with tears on my cheekbones.

12.

I wasn't a detective, but I was curious by nature, and it wasn't a fluke that the Englishman, Billy Turner, had come into my life.

What, exactly, was going on, I didn't know, but I decided I needed more answers... which was why I found myself in Detective Smithy's office in Beverly Hills.

Detective Smithy was a good cop with a bad mustache. Today, it looked even more askew than I remembered. He said, "You're back."

"I'm back."

"Let me guess. You're still a psychic?"

"Good guess."

Detective Smithy was a believer in my talents. Maybe not at first, but by the end of my last case, he had come full circle. That I made him nervous, there was no doubt. That he masked his nervousness by being a hard ass was obvious. Then again, he was a hard ass when I'd first met him, too. So, scratch that last.

"And you're here about Liz Turner," he said.

"Maybe you're the psychic one."

"Or maybe I listened to your voicemail."

"That, too," I said.

"Well, Liz is being charged with a slew of offenses, not the least of which is murder. I'm not at liberty to discuss the case with you further."

"I have just a few questions—"

"Like I said, I'm not at liberty to answer them."

"But you are at liberty to act like a dick?"

His mouth dropped open. His mustache twitched. Then again, his mustache often twitched, the way a dying rat's whiskers might. He thought long and hard about what to say next, then got up from behind his desk, crossed the small office, and shut the glass door. He came back to his desk, sat across from me, and said, "You can't call me a dick."

"I can if you're acting like one."

"Look—"

"Or maybe I make you nervous?"

"Maybe. I don't know."

"I think I make you feel uncomfortable. And you don't like anyone coming in here and making you feel uncomfortable because you're a big, bad cop."

"I'm not that big."

"No, you're not," I said. He was only an inch taller than me.

He opened his mouth to speak, and his mustache shivered in anticipation. Then he closed his mouth again, thought about what he wanted to say, and said, "I'm sorry. Can we start over?"

"Apology accepted, and yes."

Smithy's fingernails were mostly dirty and one or two were uncommonly long, especially his pinkie nail. I wasn't sure what that was all about. That he didn't appear to belong in this polished and gleaming building in Beverly Hills was without a doubt. That he was probably the best cop on the staff was a given. That he could give a shit about how he looked was another given. Maybe the biggest.

"This is an ongoing investigation, and you ain't even a cop. I'm not supposed to talk to you about any of this," said Smithy.

"But you will anyway, she says with a glimmer of hope," I said. My voice rose a little... and so did my eyebrows.

"Only if you quit talking about yourself in the third person. It's weird."

"Deal."

"Like I said, I'm not supposed to talk to you about any of this, but I figure you and I have some secrets between us anyway."

"Like the fact that I'm a witch."

He looked away and cleared his throat. Both were true signs that he was still a tad uncomfortable with calling me a witch. "Yeah. that. Just as long as we're clear."

"We're clear."

"This is what I know: Liz Turner was found at the scene of a burglary, at Gems Unlimited here in Beverly Hills. She was found standing over the shopkeeper, who'd been shot in the chest. Witnesses say she was pressing her sweater into the wound, to staunch the bleeding."

"But it didn't help."

"No," said Smithy. "The old man died en route to the hospital."

I said, "She doesn't sound like much of a killer, if she's trying to save him."

"That's the way I see it, too. Except there's no reason for her being in there after hours. Gems Unlimited is a gem wholesaler. It's located on the fifth floor of the Montgomery Building. She had no explanation for why she was there."

"He was shot with a pistol?"

"Yes."

"Did she have the gun with her?"

"Yes."

"The same gun that killed the shopkeeper?"

"Yes."

"Was there residue on her fingers?"

"You're watching too much *CSI*, and yes, she had gunpowder residue on her. A lot of it."

"So, she fired the gun?"

"She doesn't remember. It seems likely."

"Her fingerprints on the gun?"

"Yes."

"Did she own a gun?"

"No. It was registered to someone else, someone who is now deceased."

"Deceased how long ago?"

"Fifteen years ago."

"So, the gun has, presumably, traveled from person to person, illegally, for the past fifteen years."

"A safe presumption," said Smithy.

"Does the gunpowder residue match the gun?" I asked.

"No way to know for sure. There was a high particle count on her hands—which means she had recently fired a gun. But she claims she shoots at a local range, too."

"Do they rent guns there?"

"They do."

"How long does gunpowder residue stay on one's hands?"

"Longer than you would think. Weeks, sometimes."

"And the longer the time frame, the lower the particle count?" I asked.

"Right."

"How does she explain the gun?"

"She doesn't know how she got it."

"How does she explain being in the gem shop, after hours?"

"She hasn't given us a satisfactory answer. Either way, it doesn't matter. She's our only suspect. Unless you've seen something different that can change that."

"Seen?"

"Yeah, you know. With your third eye, or whatever the fuck you whackos call it."

"Whackos?" I said. "Care to rephrase that?"

"Sorry. That slipped out. I'm still a dick, remember?"

"And, I'm still a witch, remember?"

"Point taken. So, tell me, is the girl guilty or not?"

"What do you think?" I asked.

"Hey, I ain't the psychic one."

"No," I said, "but you have a keen sixth sense. Even I can see that. You trust your gut, which is a form of psychic intuition. So, what does your gut say?"

"That she did it. But something doesn't seem right."

"And what's that?"

"For one... she says she doesn't remember doing it."

"Seems like that might be a common excuse."

"Not exactly," said Smithy. "Most will say they didn't do it. Not that they didn't remember doing it. It's strange as hell."

"Does she have a mental disorder?" I asked. "Schizophrenia?"

"We're having her examined. So far, there's nothing conclusive."

"But..." I heard his voice trail off, or I sensed

there was something more that he wanted to add.

"She claims she talks to a demon of some sort."

"A demon?"

"Yeah. She says it tells her what to do."

He looked at me long and hard, and then took in a lot of air. That his mustache rippled like a caterpillar having a seizure should not have made me laugh. But it did.

Dammit.

"What's so funny?" he asked.

"Nothing, sorry. Okay, it's your mustache."

"What about my mustache?"

"It's bushy and a little crooked and sort of moves on its own sometimes."

"Yeah, so?"

"Have you considered... never mind."

"How about we stay focused on a young girl who may or may not be possessed?"

"Right, sorry." I collected myself and said, "I want to talk to her."

"I'll see what I can arrange."

13.

I was sitting crossed-legged in the center of my living room, facing north, in the direction of my big sliding glass door. Beyond the open curtains, the ritzy apartment tower across the street was veritably on fire with the setting sun, its glass façade reflecting and refracting the light.

I was practicing casting spells and mixing potions, all under the careful—and ghostly—eye of Millicent Laurie, although I doubted she used her last name much these days.

After spending nearly an hour trying to cast a money spell, I finally gave up. It wasn't that the spell itself was hard, or that the phrasing was difficult, or that it was particularly challenging to combine the various ingredients of the potion together. No, that was actually all very easy.

My problem was simple: *belief.*

I didn't *believe* in what I was doing. I didn't *believe* that doing a basic spell could create a windfall of money for me, or anyone else. Seeing into the future, seeing long distance, reading Samantha's mind... and even telekinesis... yes, all of this I could believe. I lived it each day, after all.

But money spells?

That's where I drew the line. And this was coming from someone who had seen a person turn into a giant bat. And had seen another turn into a werewolf.

Sadly, my mind drew the line at wishing for more money... and creating it.

After going through the money spell again—at Millicent's insistence—I finally tossed aside the spell book, got up, and headed into the kitchen. There, I took out a Pabst Blue Ribbon and popped open the can.

I was drinking heavily from it when I felt the hair on the back of my neck stand on end. That would be Millicent, of course. I ignored her and my erect hair follicles and kept drinking. When I was about halfway done with the beer, a mostly seethrough Millicent was now standing before me, shimmering and hovering and looking creepy as hell. She also didn't look happy.

"You lack faith, child." Her voice was whispery and faint and it appeared just inside my ear. This time, her lips didn't move. Nor did they have to.

"You think?" I said.

"Why is that?"

"Because money doesn't just appear out of thin air. You might appear out of thin air, but money doesn't."

"Some of what we do is instant, I agree. But other things—spell casting, for instance—takes time to develop. Hence, the need for faith."

"No one uses words like *hence* anymore, Millicent. Get with the times." Yes, I was feeling cranky and a little belligerent. "Besides, I make enough money to get by."

If she was offended by my little outburst, she didn't show it. She remained standing calmly in front of me, hands crossed before her. "The exercise isn't about making you more money, child. The exercise is to develop your spell-casting skills... and to develop your faith, as well."

"Well, I suppose I could use the extra money. There is, after all, a reason why I work *two* jobs." In fact, I was pretty sure I was the only person living in Beverly Hills who lived from paycheck to paycheck.

Throughout this pity party, Millicent watched me closely, rising and falling gently on currents unseen and unfelt by me. These days, Millicent appeared to me as a woman in her late thirties, maybe a little older than me. At first, she had presented herself as an older woman, as she had looked at the time of her passing. As time went on, and we got to know each other better, she appeared to be aging backward.

I knew I had major hang-ups with money. I had grown up in a low-income household, and I knew I had been holding onto the false belief that wealth was for the fortunate, the gifted, the blessed.

I knew this belief was wrong. Certainly, I deserved money as well as the next person. Hell, maybe even more so. I worked my ass off at two jobs and still drove a lame car.

No, it wasn't lame. It was a very good car that worked reliably.

"Good, child," came Millicent's words, following my train of thought. "Yes, appreciate what you have. That is a good place to start."

"Easy for you to say," I mumbled. Millicent was, after all, from a rich banking family.

"Only in the last life, child. More often than not, I struggled."

I grabbed a water bottle from the fridge and headed back to the living room. I decided to change the subject. Money always depressed me. "And you have access to all of these past lives?" I asked.

"Of course."

"But I don't."

She shook her head. "No, child. The physical life is challenging enough without access to the burdens and misfortunes and mistakes of one's past lives."

"You make it sound like I was a big mess."

"You had a lot of learning to do, Allison. You made... questionable choices."

"Did I hurt people?"

She waited before answering. "Yes."

"Did I kill people?"

She paused again before answering. "Yes."

"Jesus." I sat in the center on the living room, surrounded by my open spell books and vials of hocus-pocus ingredients. Candles burned in a semi-circle, and the statue of my animal familiar—an eagle—sat nearby. We all have an animal familiar. Mine just happened to be a bald eagle, and I couldn't have been happier. Millicent was teaching me to connect with the spirit of the eagle in my meditations. The process had been... interesting.

"Why did you hesitate before answering my question?" I asked.

Millicent's expression was unfathomable. "I was discussing your request with your spirit guide, of course."

"You are in contact with my spirit guide?" I asked.

"This surprises you, child?"

"I thought, well, *you* were my spirit guide."

She shook her head and a slow smile spread over her slightly glowing face. "No, dear. I am your friend and companion, a soul mate, if you will."

"Why did you consult with my spirit guide? And who is she?"

"He," corrected Millicent. "And it is up to him —and your higher, spiritual self—to decide what information you need to know in this present incarnation. Not all information from past lives is

beneficial in the current life."

"And he's the one deciding that?"

"He is... along with your higher self."

"Well, that just sucks."

Millicent paused before answering, and I suspected she was, once again, consulting with my spirit guide. "Consider the torment you would feel in this life if you knew what a monster you had been in a past life."

"Okay, now I'm worried. Was I that bad?"

"We all were, dear. We all have had much growing to do. In the past, you wielded great power... and sometimes misused it. You are being given a chance in this life to balance the disharmony—or karma—from past lives."

"By doing good?"

"Yes."

"What if I don't do good in this life?" I asked.

"Then we will cross that bridge when we come to it. Just know that a lot has come into place to help you in this life... to aid you, here and now."

Millicent sat before me, her knees bending, but I knew it was just a front, a ruse. She had no knees. She could have just as easily appeared to me as a beautiful ball of light energy, except, of course, it was hard for humans to relate to balls of light energy.

"You have been given great gifts, child, gifts that could help others. Witchcraft is not for personal gain, remember that. We are extensions of Mother Earth herself."

I motioned to the spell books and the vials of ingredients. "But I'm really no good at this stuff."

"Maintain your strengths," she said, reaching out and touching my hand. Energy crackled through me and around me. "And work on your weaknesses."

"That's a very zen thing to say," I said.

"Truth is truth," said Millicent.

"I *am* good at this," I said and raised my hands. As I did so, all of the spell books and vials and candles and even the eagle statue lifted into the room. I motioned my hands and the various items swirled in a slow vortex. I motioned my hands faster and the pages flapped and vials tumbled in the air, faster and faster. Wax flung far and wide throughout the room. I was going to have to clean that later.

"A nice trick, Allison."

"I know, I know," I said, lowering my hands. The items all settled in place, mostly where they had begun. "Work on my weaknesses."

"Good, child."

"And what are *your* strengths?" I asked.

"My gifts now are more spiritual in nature, Allison. But in the past, I was gifted at connecting with all of nature, from plants and animals, to even the rocks themselves. All of nature spoke to me. And still does."

I thought about that. "And Samantha Moon was our potions expert back then?"

"She was," said Millicent. "But not anymore."

"Because now she's a vampire."

"Her life—this life—has taken a different path, it's true. However, I have brought to you another."

"You mean Ivy?"

"Yes, child."

As she spoke those words, a past life was revealed to me... surely it was a scene approved by my spirit guide and higher self. In it, I saw myself in the woods with two other women... women who did not look like either Sam or Millicent... but who were still them, all the same. Indeed, I recognized their *soul imprint*. And in the shadows, in the background, watching all of this, was a young girl. She was, in fact, one of our sisters, an understudy, if you will. Waiting for her chance.

"She is strong," said Millicent when I opened my eyes again.

"But not as strong as Samantha?"

"Strong in a different way... but she is reckless."

"Aren't we all?"

"Some more than others, child. But... she is one of us. And she has been waiting for this chance."

"Do you miss her, Millie?" I asked.

"Do I miss Sam, our witch sister?"

"Yes."

The spirit thought about it, then looked away. "More than you know."

"She's still here," I said. "She's still part of my life."

"But not part of mine," said Millie. "Now, let's get back to work."

I thought about all of this as I continued working again on my spellcraft—in particular, money spells. Working, as Millicent put it, on building up my weaknesses.

So far, I hadn't won the lottery, perhaps because magic wasn't supposed to be for personal gain. Okay, so if I won, I would help a lot of people.

My weaknesses sometimes held me back.

But I'm trying.

14.

Detective Smithy made it happen.

The next afternoon, after my morning shift at The Psychic Hotline, I found myself seated across from a young woman wearing orange prisoner clothing. Separating us was ultra-thick, bullet-proof glass. Samantha Moon had once told me about her encounter with such a bulletproof piece of glass. Advantage: vampire.

Although Smithy had pulled some strings, I still had to wait nearly an hour, along with the rest of the dregs of Los Angeles. I think I might have been murdered a half dozen times—at least in the minds of those sitting around me.

Anyway, I was finally ushered into booth two, where I waited only a few minutes before a young girl appeared, blinking at me rapidly and looking generally confused.

I knew Liz Turner's face by now, thanks to the many pictures in Billy's home. I nodded encouragingly as she continued to blink uncertainly, letting her know that, yes, she had arrived at the right booth. She looked at me some more, looked back from the doorway she'd just appeared from, glanced at the guard who was making his slow rounds behind the prisoners, and then looked back at me and shrugged.

As she shrugged, I saw it, of course. It was hard to miss, after all: the same dark energy that swirled through Billy Turner's aura swirled through hers as well. Perhaps it was even darker, if that was possible.

This wasn't good; in fact, it was very, very bad. This meant she was going to die... and die rather soon.

Unless I was dead wrong.

Maybe I was wrong. Maybe I was reading people incorrectly. Maybe I didn't know what the hell I was talking about.

No. I had seen Billy's impending death—his horrible, horrible death—as he had brushed up against me at his home. True, I couldn't know for sure if Liz Turner was going to die, unless I touched her, which wasn't going to happen with this thick piece of glass between us. And, unfortunately, I wasn't a vampire who could punch my way through it. But I could make an educated guess. And my guess suggested that she was going to die... within days, if not hours.

Holy shit.

A moment later, she reached for the red phone receiver hanging on the partition that separated her from the prisoner in the booth next door. I was already holding the other one. I was proactive like that.

"Hi," I said.

"Who the hell are you?" Liz asked.

"My name's Allison Lopez."

"Who *are* you?"

"I'm a friend of your dad's," I said.

Her eyes narrowed, and as they did so, something flashed behind them, something red and menacing. "He's never talked about you before."

"I'm a new friend."

Liz Turner was twenty-four. She had her whole life ahead of her. She had, in fact, everything to live for. She lived a comfortable life in Santa Monica. So, why had she killed a shopkeeper? I was beginning to have my suspicions why, but I needed to confirm them. Liz was cute in a plain way. She had big, round eyes with naturally long lashes. She spoke with a faint English accent.

Those same round eyes were widening... her pupils were shrinking to pinpricks. Red flared just behind her pupils. I doubted that others could see the red, but I saw it, and that was all that mattered.

"Father is an unbeliever," she said.

"In what?" I asked.

The red in her eyes flared. "In me."

"And who are you?"

"We are many."

"You speak of yourself in the plural, Liz?"

"I am not Liz. Not now. Sometimes I permit her to return, but mostly, I do not. Soon, it will be time to destroy her. In this place, she is of no use to me."

"What are you?"

"I am your worst nightmare."

I almost smiled. In fact, I think I might have. "I've seen worse."

The red in her eyes flared and the darkness around her swirled, faster and faster. Now, thick, black cords wove within her dark aura. They wove and swirled and tightened. These could have been a hundred black vipers. A thousand.

"I want to speak to Liz," I said firmly.

"And I want to kill you, Allie."

Hearing the entity speak my name was unsettling at best, but I refused to show it. "Where's Liz?"

She looked at me for a long moment, and a slow smile spread over her face. "Waiting to die."

"You have possessed her."

"Never give the devil an opening."

"How did she give you an opening?" I asked.

"You ask a lot of questions, witch."

I had never spoken directly to a demon, although, at one point in my life, I, too, had been possessed. But that was another story. As I sat there, I summoned light energy to surround me. I felt it move over me and around me, and I saw it flare briefly in the eyes of Liz. She sat back a little.

"Stop it," she said.

I decided that firmness was the best approach to dealing with a demon. "Answer me," I said. "How did she let you in?"

"She had many openings, witch. Her guard was down, you could say."

I knew that, in general, dark entities could not gain access to us without either an invitation... or if our psychic guard was down. There was some disagreement as to how exactly one's psychic guard could be down, but some believed that extreme depression and drug and alcohol abuse were some ways that gave demons an invitation to possess a human.

"She was depressed?" I asked.

"Wouldn't you be?" she asked. "Living in that big, dark, creepy haunted house. So far from home. You might start taking some illegal drugs, too. Anything to... cope." It spoke that last word in a guttural whisper, and grinned broadly. Too broadly. I had seen a grin like that before, last year, on a remote island in the Pacific Northwest.

"So, you took advantage of her situation," I said. "You took advantage of a depressed girl."

"You call it taking advantage... I call it an opportunity."

"An opportunity to do what?"

"To live," she said, and her voice was quickly sounding less and less female. "It had been far too long."

"Because the house stood empty," I said.

"You are a smart witch."

"Then why kill her?" I asked. "If you need her to live?"

"Because I am working on another. You might have met him. He is close to coming around, you could say. He's fighting me, but it's always a losing fight."

I knew, of course, who he was talking about. "You would kill a father and daughter?"

"I will kill all that I can, and as many as I can, and as often as I can."

"Why?"

It looked at me oddly. "You ask too many questions, witch."

"Answer me," I said, sitting forward. I surrounded myself with even more white light, imagining it engulfing me completely, spreading down through the floor and up through the ceiling, behind me and even through the glass. Liz shrank back even further.

"Answer me," I said again. "Why do you hurt others?"

"I don't hurt them," she said, sitting back now in her chair, the phone's cord stretched to its max. "I possess them, I control them, I own them, I destroy them. Then I kill them. I do far, far worse things than hurt them."

"Why?" I asked. "Why do you do these things?"

Liz cocked her head at me, and I saw that she

had bitten down hard on her lip and maybe even her tongue. Blood spilled over her jaw and down over her orange jumpsuit.

"Fuck you, witch," she said.

15.

The city was beautiful at night.

Perhaps no more beautiful than other big cities, but I enjoyed what Beverly Hills had to offer. Big, safe streets were filled with mostly friendly people. And those who ignored you were generally on the phone or texting, but, on the off chance that you caught them mid-text, they generally looked up and smiled.

Generally.

I was walking down Third Street, surrounded by rows of elegant apartments and apartments. The buildings were a beehive of activity. Open curtains revealed couples eating, people talking, cooking, watching TV, and working out. There was movement everywhere. Cars were coming and going. I passed many joggers and dog walkers and nannies.

I was walking to clear my head and to think, which might have been counterproductive. I was wearing a light windbreaker and a white beanie cap. No, it wasn't *that* cold, but my ears got cold easily. I hated when my ears got cold. I wore yoga pants and sneakers, and, I suspected, I looked kinda cute. Maybe not.

It was hard to think about being cute—or anything else, for that matter—when death and demons were on your mind.

Yes, I had some experience with demons. In fact, I had some very personal experience with a "body-hopping" demon on a remote island in the Pacific Northwest. It was personal because I just happened to be a blood relative of a cursed family... and I got to experience first-hand just what it felt like to have another entity control my body. I had watched from the depths of my own mind—as if from a nightmare—as another creature literally took control of my body. Moving me, walking me, speaking for me.

At the time, I could do nothing more than watch passively. It was terrible, and I wouldn't have wished the experience on my worst enemy.

I had done nothing to invite the entity in. I had simply had the misfortune of being a distant relative of a family who was very, very cursed.

However, Billy and his daughter weren't cursed. The house was cursed. The land was cursed. And Lord help anyone who came into contact with either, let alone anyone who lived there.

I didn't know what to do for either of them. That they were both on a path of destruction, there was no doubt. The blackness that invaded their auras wasn't the demon. It was looming death. Imminent death.

I walked faster, tucking my hands in my jacket pockets. My friend, Samantha, had destroyed that demon last year. But that had been different. So different. An ancient family member had invited the demon in... a family member who had lived on until it had decided to take on Samantha.

No, I thought suddenly. It hadn't been a demon. It had been a highly evolved dark master. It had been someone who had once been human, but no more. Someone who had elevated their status through wicked means.

Not a demon, I thought. A human who acted like a demon. There was a difference.

The thing I had seen in Billy's house had never been human. I was sure of it. Its very essence was so... foreign.

I shuddered and continued on, wondering what to do about Billy and Liz, and who to speak to, but knowing the answers would come soon.

They had to.

Time was running out.

***

A half hour later, lost in dark thoughts, I

rounded a corner and stepped onto Rodeo Drive. I admired shop after shop, window display after window display, of some of the most famous brand names: Gucci, Valentino, Versace, Ralph Lauren, Jimmy Choo, Giorgio Armani, Cartier, Bulgari, Chanel, Prada, Fendi, and so many more.

I sighed heavily, as I usually did.

And, as usual, a sense of despondency overcame me. And not just because I had seen my first demon. These shops weren't for me, I knew that. They were for other people, rich people, successful people. People who'd figured out the money enigma.

Not me. No, I had just enough to get through the week, until my next check.

I knew money didn't just magically grow on trees. Millicent said it was a process of abundance coming to me. Not necessarily money. She'd also said for me to have faith. To keep that door open, and to not shut it firmly.

"Easier said than done," I mumbled, as I passed Céline's storefront, sighing at the rows of shoes and handbags.

Yes, I knew that my attitude, even now, was shutting that door firmly. But how to open it? That was the question.

I took in a lot of air, and did what I had read in one of those *Law of Attraction* books on money. I visualized myself spending imaginary money. I imagined walking into these stores and spending money I didn't have. Mostly, I imagined what it would feel like to *have* money. And for a few minutes, as I stopped before the Jimmy Choo shop and gazed at the latest shoe offerings, it felt heavenly. And, I had to admit, for a few brief minutes, I was about to capture that wonderful feeling of having abundance... and having exactly what I wanted.

Then I sighed... and continued on.

Fat lot of good that did me.

The shoes were still in the shop and I was still barely making it. I sighed again, and continued home.

I did, after all, have the evening shift at The Psychic Hotline.

My life.

16.

I cut short my shift when I got a call from Detective Smithy.

No, my bosses at the Hotline wouldn't be happy my line was busy. They could also suck it.

Now, we were in my apartment. I was having wine, and plenty of it, especially after the day I'd had. Detective Smithy declined, saying he never drank when on duty. I told him we were talking about demons and possessions and were in my apartment, and tried to convince him that he was hardly on official duty. Smithy mentioned that he was never off-duty, and he was always working cases, even in the shower. I thanked him for that visual.

His arrival at my house had been unexpected. I

hadn't bothered to straighten my house after buzzing him in. Anyone with a mustache like his wouldn't care about dishes in my sink, or jeans over the backs of my dining room chairs.

Now we sat in my living room. He was on the couch. I was in one of my straight-back chairs. He was still wearing his cop uniform; that is, the long-sleeved shirt and boring slacks. He was rumpled, of course. Always rumpled. I was in jeans and a tee-shirt, and not so rumpled.

"They have Liz Turner under a suicide watch," he said.

"A good idea, but I don't think it will work."

"What do you mean?"

"It's going to kill her, Detective."

"When you say 'it,' do you mean the demon?"

"Yes."

"And how would 'it' kill her?"

"My guess? Probably creatively."

"And how..." Smithy struggled for words. He sat forward on the couch. His shoes were mostly unpolished and scuffed. "How on earth could it kill her?"

"It has complete control of her."

"But how?"

"Possession. You've seen the movies."

He stood suddenly, ran his fingers through his thick hair. He was a short man with thick legs. He paced before the couch. "But this isn't a movie, Allison. Demons don't possess people in the real world."

"Then you don't live in the same world where I live, Detective."

"But how is it possible? I don't understand."

"There are worlds layered over ours. Higher and lower dimensions. Whatever you want to call it. But there is an unseen world that mostly stays unseen. Unless..."

"Unless what, dammit?"

"Unless someone opens a doorway of some type."

Smithy digested this, and then sat on the couch again. "We have Liz Turner's psychiatric test results. She's a paranoid schizophrenic. She's one of the most extreme examples the jail psychiatrist had ever seen. You name it: delusions, paranoia, hallucinations."

"Or possession," I said, cutting him off. "I wasn't talking to the girl. I was talking to the thing that possessed her."

"A demon?"

"It called itself 'the devil' at some point, but I think it was being melodramatic."

"Oh, God. This isn't happening."

"Denial doesn't suit you, Detective."

He ran a palm over his forehead and cheeks, the picture of a man grappling with the Great Unknown. When he was done having his little cop temper tantrum, he finally looked at me. He didn't look good. He looked... defeated. There was nothing about this case that he was trained to cope with. Hell, there was nothing about this case anyone was trained to cope with. Except, maybe, an exorcist.

"I did some research on Billy Turner's house," he finally said, sitting back. He looked like a man who needed a drink.

"Oh?"

"I went down through the records of the last six owners since the place was first built. Took me all day today."

"Sounds like a good use of a homicide detective's time."

"Not really. There's going to be hell to pay later, trust me. But, until then, I uncovered some information."

"Lay it on me."

I expected the detective to take out a notepad, but I was wrong. He had, apparently, logged all the information away in his noggin. "Seven owners... seven violent deaths. Four of them suicides. Two of them in the house."

"And the other two?"

"In prison."

"Prison for what?"

"Murder. In fact, Billy Turner and his daughter, Liz Turner, are the only living owners, past or present, of the house on Mockingbird Lane."

"And they won't be for long," I said.

"Unless we do something about it?" he said.

I shook my head. "I don't think there's anything we can do, detective."

"What about removing the demon?"

"Did a Beverly Hills homicide detective just ask

me about removing a demon?"

"I did, and cut the shit. I'm doing my best to wrap my brain around this. What if we removed the demon? Would that save the two of them?"

"Maybe," I said. "But..."

"But their damn auras, right?"

I nearly asked again if a Beverly Hills homicide detective just said the word "aura," but I let it go. Instead, I said, "Yeah. Their auras are black. Totally black."

"And black means death?"

"Right."

"And this is irreversible?"

"Mostly." I decided not to mention Samantha Moon saving her own son from the brink of death.

"Any idea where this demon came from?"

"Hard to say," I said. "But my best guess is that it's been living in that house, or on that land, for some time."

"Possessing and killing anyone who lives there."

"Right," I said.

"I'm not afraid of it," said Smithy suddenly.

"You should be," I said.

"I'm not," he said again.

I gave him a half smile. "Good, because neither am I."

17.

When the good detective was gone, after he'd made me promise that I wouldn't do anything stupid, I did the only non-stupid thing I could think of: I called Billy Turner.

"Hi, Allison." He sounded far cheerier than the last time I had spoken with him.

"I hope I didn't catch you at a bad time," I said, and as I spoke, I logged into him. It took a moment, but soon, I saw him clearly enough. He was in his house, walking slowly through the main downstairs hallway. There were no portraits on the wall. They were blank and dark. In fact, the whole house was dark.

There was just enough ambient light from his cell phone, and streetlights, for me to see him moving through his home. Mostly, though, he was in shadow.

"Are you okay, Billy?" I asked.

"I couldn't be better, Allison. Why do you ask?"

I decided to lay all my cards on the table. After all, even with minimal light, I could see that the shadow around Billy had darkened considerably since the last time I had seen him.

"You're walking around in the dark, Billy."

"You can see me?"

"Yes, I can."

"But how? Are you here with me?"

"In a way, yes."

"Where am I, if you don't mind me asking?"

"You're nearing the end of your hallway. In fact, you just turned and are walking back through the hallway."

"Very good, Allison. You are an astonishingly talented psychic."

"Billy, you need to leave this house."

"Why, Allie? Do you mind if I call you Allie?"

I ignored him. I was very, very dismayed to hear his voice changing, picking up a guttural cadence I was already familiar with, a sound and quality I heard coming from his daughter.

"Please, Billy. You need to leave. The house..."

"The house is what, Allie?"

Was I speaking with Billy or the demon? I couldn't tell. Billy was still there, though. I heard it in his voice. The demon had said Billy was still resistant. Then again, could I trust a demon?

"Billy, listen to me. You need to leave the house. It's not safe there."

As he walked, Billy reached out and ran a hand along one of the walls. "I love it here, Allie. It's my posh dream home, you know. I always wanted to live and work near Hollywood. Now, I'm making movies and living the dream. Life is brill."

"Brill?" I asked.

"Brilliant. Excellent."

Billy's voice was intermixed with the demon's. It varied from an English accent... to something deeper and angrier.

"It has no power over you, Billy. You can still fight it."

"Fight what, Allie?"

"You know what, Billy."

"I want to hear you say it, witch."

"The demon, Billy. The thing living in your house, haunting your house, possessing your house. And you and Liz."

He laughed loudly, pausing in the hallway. As he did so, I watched shadows crawling along his walls. Clawed shadows. Horned shadows. They swarmed along the walls.

"Please, Billy. You must leave."

He dropped to his knees. The phone dropped before him, too, clattering over the floor. I heard him weeping.

"I fought it for so long, Allie. I tried to resist. But watching my daughter collapse, watching her descend into darkness, madness... it was too much. I don't care anymore, Allie. Without her, I have nothing. And now she's gone to jail. She's going to go to prison..."

"Billy!"

But he wasn't listening. I watched him roll onto his side, and curl into the fetal position, right there in the hallway, and as he did so, the shadows came down from the walls and moved over the floor... and swarmed over him.

Over him, and around him, and through him.

"No!" I screamed.

18.

"I like Detective Smithy," said Millicent while I was trying to calm myself after my disturbing phone call with Billy Turner.

"So do I."

"But he will be of no help to us, child. Only witches, or something more powerful, can save Billy Turner now."

I nodded. I knew that. The detective was barely a believer. And he had no experience in the supernatural.

"I hated seeing what happened to Billy tonight while we spoke on the phone. I should go over there. Fight that thing. Get Billy out of the house."

"You must rest tonight, recharge your batteries and let the answers come to you. You cannot fight a demon when you are fighting sleep."

I realized she was right. I was exhausted and in no shape to deal with a demon tonight. "Can the demon even be defeated?" I asked.

"Of course."

"But how?"

We were in the kitchen, but as I spoke, I headed into my bedroom, which was down a short hall and to the left. In the blink of an eye, my clothing was off and the most comfy pajamas I could imagine were on. Moments later, I was in bed, hugging my favorite pillow. Lying across from me was a dead woman.

She waited for me to get comfy before speaking. "I don't know, child."

"What do you mean, you don't know? You're dead. You have access to all of the knowledge in the spirit world."

"I am limited to what I can show you. But that is not the case here."

"What is the case here?" I asked. My eyes were getting heavy, although I wasn't sure I wanted to sleep. How did one sleep just hours after speaking to an honest-to-God demon through the mouth of a possessed Englishman? I didn't know. I suspected sleep would come in fits and starts, if at all.

"I do not know how to vanquish a demon, child."

"The triad has never done it in the past?"

"No, Allison."

"Well, shi—oot."

Yes, I barely caught myself, although Millicent still frowned a little. Having a ghost lying by me in bed, frowning at my near-use of a semi-foul word should have been surreal and frightening, but I guess even I was finally getting used to it. But barely. The hairs on my arms were still standing on end. I didn't think my natural reaction to ghosts would ever go away.

"Maybe we shouldn't worry about vanquishing the demon and all that. Let's just convince the city to tear down the home. Maybe it will just, you know, go away," I said hopefully. I was getting even sleepier.

"You're grasping at straws because you fear to face the demon. You know that is not the answer, child."

"What is the answer?" I asked, feeling a sick dread come over me.

"This experience was brought to you to grow, to learn from, and to help another. More importantly, I suspect this situation was brought to you, specifically, to help rid the Earth of this creature."

"There's so much I don't understand," I said.

"There is much to learn, child."

"But this thing is so... dangerous."

"And so are we, child."

"You will help me?" I asked.

"Of course. Myself, and one other."

"Ivy," I said. It wasn't a question.

"Yes, child."

"It doesn't seem right to call her up and ask

what she's up to, then see if she's free to help us destroy a demon."

"She is reckless and wild and more than up for this little adventure," said Millicent.

"Okay," I said drowsily. "I'll give her a call tomorrow."

What I didn't add was: I hope it's not too late.

"Good," said Millicent. "But first—"

I cut her off. "But first, we need to know how to destroy the demon."

"Yes, child."

I grinned. "I might know someone who has an idea."

And with that, my eyes closed and the static electricity in the room, energy created by the ghost of Millicent, faded away, too.

I slept like a baby.

A baby who dreamed of monsters and shadows and things that went bump in the night.

Sigh.

19.

He was called The Librarian.

At least, that's what Samantha Moon called him. What he was, exactly, was anyone's guess. However, Sam had informed me that, more than likely, he was on the side of good... and that was good enough for me. She also told me he might have answers for me. And that was even better.

Mostly, she'd warned me I might never find him. She'd said the Librarian—whose real name was Archibald Maximus, which was about the fanciest name I'd ever heard—didn't always reveal himself. She'd said only those who were ready could find him. She'd said even those looking for the Occult Room on the third floor of the Cal State Fullerton Library would never find it.

That sounded like a challenge, so, of course, I headed over there.

In fact, when I asked the clerk at the library help desk downstairs how to find the Occult Room, she only shrugged and said she'd never heard of it.

I frowned at that, and then headed over to the elevators, and pressed the button to the third floor. When the door opened, I followed Sam's instructions and headed to the west wall, away from where many students were working. I looked for a side room, an annex, as Sam had called it.

There was nothing there. Just one, long empty wall. I walked along it, searching, running my hand over it. I did the only thing I could think of; I asked Millicent to intercede for me, to seek out this Librarian and let him know that I needed help. I reached the end of the hallway, and turned back.

Where there had been nothing but a blank wall, there was now a door along the west wall, an arched opening with the words "OCCULT READING ROOM" over the top.

I think my mouth might have dropped open.

I took in a lot of air, headed back down the hallway, and hung a right into the reading room, noting that my heart was beating faster than it had in some time.

***

The Occult Reading Room didn't look like something out of Hogwarts, or like something that might have been found in Dracula's castle. There weren't paintings whose eyes—or even faces— turned to watch me as I walked past. And the Librarian wasn't a grizzled old wizard with a long beard and twinkle in his eye.

No, the Librarian was a young man, dressed smartly in a trim suit—it was a generic suit that seemed timeless and could have, in fact, been from any number of designers. Either way, it fit him perfectly. His smile was warm. His eyes were bright. His hair was neat and trim and his fingers were long and strong. He could have been a college student working in the Occult Reading Room, except that he wasn't. *What* he was, I still didn't know.

"Can I help you?" he asked. He was a little too aware, too in control of himself and his every movement, and his accent was nearly impossible to place.

"Yes, I hope you can."

He smiled warmly, and watched my every move behind bright eyes. "I shall do my best."

Samantha told me she thought Archibald Maximus—who looked nothing like an Archibald Maximus, I might add, was an alchemist, as in, someone who was a true master of potions. In my mind, this made him a bit of a wizard, but what did I know? Samantha also thought he was part of a bigger network of those who battled evil. Or, as Maximus had put it to her a while ago, he and others like him were to balance the dark with the light.

Who knew for sure, but earlier today, after discussing with Sam what I might be dealing with, she had thought it best that I head out to Orange County... and find Maximus for some real answers. And now, here I was.

"Samantha Moon suggested that I talk with you," I said boldly.

He nodded, smiling.

"She also suggested that there was a very good chance I would never find you, and I almost didn't. I walked right past it."

"Most don't see it, it's true. Funny what happens when you simply... ask to be shown the way."

I could only nod.

He went on, "Just imagine what other mysteries are waiting to be revealed."

"I-I suppose so."

"Now, how can I help you, Allison?"

"I..." I closed my mouth. "I didn't tell you my name."

"And I didn't tell you mine either," he said. "And yet you know it."

"This is weird," I said.

"Isn't it?"

"But Sam told me your name."

"And Millicent told me yours. We're even, I guess."

"So weird," I said.

"We've established that," he said, winking. "Now, let's see if I can help you."

***

I caught him up on what I knew about Billy and Liz, and the demon in their house.

Hard to know if the Librarian already knew what I was talking about, or if this was new information. He gave away little, and revealed even less. No doubt that the young man standing across the help desk was an enigma. That he might not be a young man at all, but a very old soul, was the question. Well, one of the questions.

When I finished telling him about it, he said, "You have seen this entity, you say?"

I nodded. "When I was at their home. It was sort of creeping down a hallway, watching us."

"And you saw it in the young lady's aura, as well?"

"Yes."

"Would you mind if I accessed these two memories, so that I can have a better understanding of what we're dealing with?"

"Access?" I asked. The word might have come out a little squeakier than I'd intended.

"Yes, I will ask you to remember these two events again, while I briefly slip into your thoughts. It's not dissimilar to the connection you have with Sam. But mine will be brief and only this one time."

"Okay," I said. "But I'm going to warn you. It's cluttered in there."

"No problem." He smiled warmly and gestured

for me to come closer to him, which I did, leaning on my hands over the counter.

"This isn't going to hurt," he said.

"Good to know."

He reached over and placed his palms on either side of my head, just above my ears, holding me gently.

"I bet you do this with all the girls," I said.

"Only psychic witches who have seen a very rare, and very old, entity."

I had opened my mouth for another sassy comeback, but his words shut me right up. I closed it again, and couldn't escape the fact that my heart was now thumping loudly just inside my eardrums.

"Okay, Allie. I want you to think back to the first time you saw the creature. Just go back to that moment in your mind."

His touch was not unpleasant. That I couldn't hear him breathing was slightly unsettling. Samantha rarely, if ever, breathed, either. And if she did, it was only to appear normal... and only when she remembered to do it. Her touch, however, was ice cold. His was warm, gentle... and soothing. I decided I liked his touch.

Hi, Allie.

The words manifested just inside my ear, in the same place where I "heard" Samantha Moon talking to me.

Fancy meeting you *hear*, I thought, joking around with him.

He smiled at me. *Now, think back to the first*

111

time, please... and I'm glad you like my touch.

I felt my face heat up as I closed my eyes. I cast my thoughts back to my meeting with Billy, when I had been sitting with him on the couch, and when I had been looking down the hallway.

As I thought this, my mind strayed to Archibald's touch again, his warmth, and the way he gently cradled my head in his hands... and I lost all focus. I opened my eyes and smiled shyly at him.

"Um, sorry," I said.

"No reason to be sorry," he said softly, giving me a crooked smile.

I closed my eyes, and decided I liked his smile, too. "Let me try again."

Please do, came his silent words, *and I like your smile, as well.*

Uh-oh, I thought, and sensed him smile.

I did what I was asked, and focused all my thoughts on the scene at Billy's house. When I felt my thoughts stray, I reined them back in. I replayed the memory as best as I could, and did it over and over again.

Good, Allison. Now, show me what you saw with the daughter.

I nodded as he continued holding my head. I would have expected him to breathe on me. His face was, after all, just a few inches from mine. A handsome face.

Dammit. I felt the heat spring to my face, knowing he had just picked up on my stray thought.

I am flattered, came his gentle words.

I took in a lot of air, and this time, replayed the events as I'd seen them at the jail, as the darkness clouded Liz's aura, as we'd done our best to try to banish it, only to see a trailing darkness remain. I repeated the scene again, over and over, quickly, until he released my head.

"Ah," he said, settling back into his space behind the help desk.

"What, exactly, does *ah* mean?" I asked.

He pulled at his small goatee on his narrow chin. While I waited, I saw something curious from the back of the Occult Reading Room, where thousands upon thousands of books crowded the bookshelves. I saw a slow darkness appear from one of the books. The darkness swirled briefly, took the vague form of a human shape, and then returned to the book. What, exactly, that was, I didn't know, but the Librarian didn't seem concerned. As I continued waiting for Archibald Maximus to mull over what he had seen in my head, I realized almost all of the books in this collection emitted a dark energy. I couldn't always see the energy, not like the swirling dark mist, but I felt it, and, if I listened hard enough, I could almost seem to hear it. Whispering, rattling, chanting...

So weird.

When Archibald was done pulling his sparse chin hair, he looked sideways at me. I was slightly dismayed to see the twinkle in his eye was gone, replaced with a look of deadly seriousness.

"Yes, I know what you're dealing with."

"Do I even want to know?"

"Probably not, but do not fear it. It thrives off of fear... and blood."

"Sounds like a vampire. Well, at least some vampires."

"In a way, it is," said Archibald. "But it's not."

"What is it?" I asked. "I'm ready. Lay it on me. Wait. Hold on. Okay, now I'm ready."

"It's a demon. Perhaps one of the oldest I've seen."

I opened my mouth to speak. I'd fully intended for some words to come out, but none came to mind, so I just stood there with my mouth hanging open.

"Unlike the highly evolved dark masters—one of which presently lives within Samantha Moon—this creature is far older and far more powerful."

"How old? And how powerful?" I asked.

"It was never human, so its age would be hard to determine, but it has the ability to control others, to get them to do its bidding."

"Like kill for it?" I asked.

"Yes, I'm afraid so. But there is another factor."

I nodded. I knew of this other factor. I had sensed it for a few days now, and with just this small prompting from Maximus, I knew where he was going with this "other factor."

"The souls who have died there are trapped there, aren't they?"

"Yes," said Maximus, seemingly impressed. "And not just those who have died there."

I nodded again, knowing where this was going. "And other victims related to those in the house."

"Of which there are many, Allison. Many who have not been reported. There is much death surrounding this house. And it is full of lost spirits."

"Lord help me."

The Librarian tapped his long fingers on the help desk counter. His tapping made all of this seem very real, that he wasn't, say, a figment of my imagination. Or, perhaps, a ghost who haunted the library. Tapping fingers created physicality. At least, I hoped it did. More interesting was all the bright gold he wore: rings and bracelets. I asked him about the gold.

He said, "Gold has very, very special qualities. Humans do not use it correctly. They use it for flash, to display wealth. In reality, gold provides great healing and protection. If more people wore pure gold against their skin, there would be far less sickness and disease in the world."

"Good thoughts," I said, "except that pure gold costs a lot of money."

"True," he said. "Except if you're an alchemist."

"What, exactly, does that mean?"

He motioned to my sterling silver ring. "Would you mind?"

"No, of course not." I slipped it off and handed it to him.

I had purchased the ring from a street vendor in Cabo two years ago. I doubted it was even pure silver, but it made me smile every time I looked at it. Good times.

The Librarian placed the ring in the center of his right palm. His hands, I noted were beyond smooth. Almost freakishly smooth. He then placed his left hand over his right and closed his eyes. I waited for a flash or for him to mumble an ancient incantation. But he mumbled nothing and there were no pyrotechnics. Instead, a moment later, he lifted his left hand, and there, sitting in his palm, was my same ring, complete with the same white stone.

But now, the tarnished silver was shining bright gold.

"Pure gold," he said. "99.999 percent gold. You would be well advised to wear it always."

"I... I will."

I slipped it on my right ring finger. It felt... warm to the touch.

"Okay," I said. "Now, what do we do about this demon?"

The Librarian grinned. "I thought you would never ask."

20.

I was in my Spirit Chair.

But not really. My body was certainly sitting comfortably, breathing easily, but in my mind, I was on a desert dune, sitting cross-legged with the beautiful woman I knew to be Mother Earth. She was a woman who wasn't a woman at all but the spirit of the very Earth we all lived on.

"Good evening, Allison," she said.

Except, of course, where we were looked like bright day. Still, it was evening back in Beverly Hills, which seemed as remote and distant as the moon and stars at this point.

A hot wind blasted over us, kicking up sand. Sand that felt real to me. Gaia smiled warmly at me —a true mother in every sense of the word.

"Good evening, Mother," I said. "Is it okay if I

address you as 'Mother'?"

"Of course, child."

I nearly made a joke about her addressing me as 'child,' but her address, much like Millicent's, was so natural, so warm, so loving, that I treasured it... and needed it, too.

I basked briefly in her presence, in her love for me, for all things on Earth, and, a moment or two later, I started my questions along that line of thinking:

"Is it true that you love all things upon Earth?"

"More than you know."

"Even those who do evil upon your surface?"

"Are you asking if I love less because one of you has made a poor choice?"

"Maybe."

The wind whipped her long, red hair, and ruffled her white gown. She looked, to me, like an Atlantean princess.

"I feel great sadness, yes, but I do not always have access to the reasons behind such choices. I only feel the effects, the blood spilled, the fear, the anger, the horror that is forever imprinted on my surface."

As she spoke, I had a mild epiphany. "You only have access to the minds of those who call on you."

"This is true. I am not the Creator, child. I am a creation, much like you. Only the Creator has access to all thoughts, desires and motivations."

I thought about that as the wind picked up. I was surprised to see that I was wearing a similar white robe. Back home, in the Spirit Chair, I was wearing jean shorts and a UCLA sweatshirt. Overhead, flashing across the sun-filled sky, was a soaring eagle. I heard its cry. I could also feel its need for nourishment. Mostly, I sensed its connection to the woman sitting across from me. It was at ease, content, free, hungry, yes, but never worried about finding food. I sensed its great trust in her... and in itself.

"It is often a relief to slip into the minds of the animals," said Gaia, following my train of thought, no doubt. "There is a beautiful simplicity and contentment... and life. So much life. It is a pleasure to fly with them, run with them, hunt with them, howl with them, swim with them, and connect with them."

"And with humans?" I asked.

She smiled at me. "Humans are a whole different animal, child. Humans are often full of angst and self-doubt and worry and fear and hate."

"You prefer communing with animals?" I asked.

"It is a nice change of pace, certainly. But they are generally as evolved as they always will be."

"I don't understand."

"Their growth is limited. Whereas, humans... well, humans' growth is limitless."

"Why is that?"

"It is the way of the Creator, child. I did not make the rules, as you humans say."

"Were you ever human?" I asked.

"No."

She gave me an image of her purpose... and it was to give life, a soul to this planet. It was a great honor for her. She had, after all, been doing this for a very long time.

"You have truly seen it all," I said. "Kingdoms rising and falling. You know all mysteries and all secrets."

She smiled at that. "A fair assessment."

I nearly asked her who had killed Kennedy, or if Bigfoot was real. As the thoughts flitted through my mind, I waved them off with a small smile.

"Some mysteries should remain a mystery," said Gaia gently. "And with some mysteries, you already know the answers."

I nodded, felt the heat on my neck, and wondered if where I was sitting was a real place, or, somehow, a dream state. I wondered if the eagle was real, too. I also realized it didn't matter if it was real or not. It felt real, and that was good enough for me.

"You allow great evil to walk on your surface," I said, finally speaking that which was troubling me the most.

"And also great good," said Gaia. "At this time, both must be here. I am merely acting as host to a greater experiment."

"Experiment?"

"Yes, child. You have been given free will to see what you will do with it. It is a great and noble experiment."

"I can't imagine that you're very pleased with the results."

"Humankind has fallen far, true, and there is the potential for total collapse. But there is also the potential for massive leaps in evolution. Positive leaps."

"You do not know which direction we will take?"

"I have seen the potentialities, child. That is all. I am ever hopeful that humankind will choose the noble path."

"And, if not?"

"Then the experiment will have failed. And it will start again."

"How many times has it failed in the past?"

She shook her head. "This information is not important to you now, child. But it has happened in the past. Often."

"Is there any hope for us now?"

"Oh, yes. The future could be bright."

I took in a lot of hot air and slipped my fingers into the soft sand. I let the grains fall away through my fingers.

I said, "I need to remove a great evil from the Earth. From you. Is that possible?"

"All things are possible."

"But you just said that evil is, well, necessary."

"Indeed, child. That is, until it is decided not to be necessary."

"Well, I am deciding that this evil is not necessary. I am deciding it is a great blight on your surface, and should be removed."

"Then so be it, child."

21.

The knock was confident, urgent.

I opened the front door, knowing full well who would be there, since I had just buzzed her in.

"Are you okay, Allie?" Ivy Tanner asked as she swept into my small apartment. I had spent the past fifteen minutes straightening it up. I wanted to make a good impression on her, although maybe it was silly to worry about the condition of the apartment.

"Yes, everything's okay."

"You said you wanted to talk. It sounded so urgent." She shivered at that, and I saw her skin prickle on her forearm. A psychic hit. "Something is up, something important."

"Yeah, you could say that."

"Does it involve our special talents?"

"It could, yeah."

Ivy was, of course, more than aware of what I could do. But she wasn't aware of much more than that. I thought about how to tell her, and then decided to tell her everything I knew. If she was going to be part of our triad, well, there were no secrets in the triad. At least, I didn't think there should be.

So, I sat her on the couch. She wanted some wine, but I suggested water instead. So, we sat with two glasses of ice water as I told her my tale. I told her about my vampire companion years ago, who was killed in his sleep, and who had first awakened my psychic gifts. Then I told her about Samantha Moon. I reminded her Samantha Moon was still very much alive and wouldn't like it much if Ivy gave away her secret. And, if she did, she should expect a visit from Samantha herself. She agreed to keep her story quiet. That is, if she really believed me. Mostly, she just stared at me with a look of growing excitement in her eyes.

Then I told her about Millicent, and about the triad, and about how we were short one witch, now that Samantha Moon had, well, switched teams. At that point, Ivy suggested we were, in fact, short *two* witches, as Millicent was presently dead. I reminded her dead witches were just as powerful, perhaps even more so. I explained Millicent had access to me and others instantly, which was never a bad thing, unless she scared the shit out of me in the shower, which she had done *once*.

"Why are you telling me all of this?" asked Ivy.

"I think you know why," I said.

She looked down at her glass of water. The rim was smudged with her lipstick. She swirled the ice, her fingers long and thin, nails perfectly manicured. Her hair looked as if she recently had it done. The quintessential rising Hollywood actor.

"Are you asking me to join you and Millicent? As a witch? In a triad?"

"Is that something you might be interested in?" I asked.

"Oh, yes! But..." She paused for dramatic effect, and I suspected this was a common ploy of hers; perhaps one could never take the actor out of her.

"But what?" I asked.

"I'm not sure I believe in all of this. Vampires? Werewolves? Ghosts? That's a lot to take in. My head is sort of spinning here. I mean, a part of me believes that this is an elaborate practical joke."

"Like a hidden-camera, reality TV show?"

"Yes, right. MTV perhaps?" She put down the glass of ice water.

I nodded. It was perfectly reasonable for her to believe that, except that she had seen me perform a trick or two before her. A trick or two that could have been staged. Faked. Her aura, I saw, was green. Green meant that she was on guard. At least, that's what I knew it to mean.

"It's not a ruse and not a reality show. What do I need to do to convince you that it's one hundred percent real?" I asked.

"Can I see Millicent?" said Ivy.

I grinned. "That's up to her, but I'll tell you right now, she's been sitting next to you this entire time."

Despite herself, Ivy gasped, her hand shooting to her chest. "I-I don't see her."

"She just put a hand on your knee," I said. "She's smiling at you. Do you feel her?"

"I-I don't know."

"Hold out your hand," I said. "And close your eyes."

Ivy did so, and I saw that it shook. Millicent, my old friend—a friend from different lives, different times who was indeed sitting next to her, took her hand. My enhanced psychic sensitivities, thanks mostly to my close association with two different vampires, allowed me to see her easily enough. Ivy, although not as psychic as me, sensed Millicent. I knew because the color of her aura changed from green to a light orange.

"You feel her," I said. "Don't you?"

Ivy made no movement. Then, her hand opened and closed. Millicent now gripped Ivy's corporeal hand in both of her ethereal hands. Ivy shivered. Her aura now rippled with a light blue. As Millicent sat with her, I knew she drew energy from her. Such energy would allow Millicent to make a full appearance.

Which she was doing now.

Little did Ivy know that a spirit was materializing next to her. Or perhaps, she did know.

More and more of her hair was standing on end.

"She's sitting next to me now, isn't she?" said Ivy. "I can feel the couch sinking. And I'm cold."

"If I said yes, would you be afraid?" I asked.

"No." Ivy shook her head, eyes still closed. "I see ghosts and spirits all the time. I know there is more to this world than the visible."

"Then open your eyes," I said.

She did, and despite her promise, Ivy screamed anyway.

22.

It was later.

Ivy was still here. She hadn't run out screaming as I thought she might. She jumped straight from the couch to the middle of the living room, where she continued screaming until I wrapped my arms around her.

Then she wept nearly hysterically, and apologized over and over. I reminded her that no one could predict how she would react to a spirit, especially one that materialized next to her, holding her hand.

Later, after a glass of wine, she calmed down enough. Millicent, to her credit, remained in the room. Trial by fire. Meaning, Ivy was just going to have to get damn well used to seeing a spirit, if she was going to be a member of our triad.

Now Ivy and I sat together on my coffee table, as Millicent remained seated on the couch. She was not really seated on the couch. Millicent was, in fact, rising and falling faintly. She only assumed the position of sitting for our benefit. Hell, she could have just as easily been standing in the couch... or hovering near the ceiling.

As Ivy calmed down, and her swirling, agitated aura calmed as well, I filled her in on Billy Turner and the demon whose name I believed might be "Baal."

"How do you know his name?"

"I'm pretty sure I know it from another lifetime. I'm thinking we have met before," I dared to tell her.

I was certain this last disclosure would drive her to leave, and for her to drop me as her personal trainer as well. But I was wrong. As I spoke, Ivy's eyes hardened and her grip on my forearm tightened.

"You don't have to do this," I said.

"No, I want to. I want to help. This thing can't keep hurting people. It's not right. It has to go."

I blinked at her words, surprised. She was, after all, the same woman who nearly peed herself at seeing the ghost of a woman. How would she fare against a murderous demon? I didn't know. But there was only one way to find out.

"So, what do we have to do?" she asked.

"You're sure you want to do this?"

"Yes," she said. "I've dreamed of this day my whole life. Well, maybe not the day I would fight a demon, but the day I would meet my soul sisters. Little did I know that one of them worked for the Psychic Hotline and as a personal trainer, and that one of them was dead."

Truth was, I was still uncomfortable with Millicent's presence. Yes, I was getting more and more used to her, but I was surprised to discover how quickly Ivy acclimated to the spirit, who faded in and out of sight.

"And your friend really is a vampire?" she asked.

"Yes."

"Can I meet Samantha Moon someday? I am, after all, taking her place in the triad, right?"

"Right. And, I'm sure you will meet her someday."

"Will she be mad that you told me her big secret?"

"Furious."

Ivy grinned and rubbed my arm. "But she'll let it go. She will understand. Say, do you think she would ever, you know, feed from me? It wouldn't hurt to have own psychic abilities enhanced, as well."

Oddly jealous, I said, "We'll see."

"Well, I can't imagine she's too picky. She's a vampire, for Christ's sake. Blood is blood, right?"

I wasn't sure if I should be offended by her words, but decided to let it go. All of this was, I knew, new for her. She was undoubtedly over-whelmed by it all. Yeah, I was going with that.

"She's excited," came Millicent's speech, directly into my head.

She's bugging me, I thought back.

"Be patient. She is young and full of fire. Besides, we will need her for tonight's work."

Tonight?

"Yes, child. The time has come."

Ivy clapped. "What are you two talking about? I can hear something, but not quite. It's a sort of murmuring just inside my ear."

I shook my head. "Is nothing sacred?"

Millicent chuckled. "Patience."

"There you two go again. I hope you're not talking about me," Ivy said.

"Nothing bad," I said.

"The two of you can speak telepathically?" she asked.

"We can," I admitted.

Ivy clapped. "Oh, cool! I can't wait to try that! So what do we do now?"

"We destroy a demon," I said.

"And then we can practice telepathy?"

I couldn't help but laugh. "One thing at a time."

My phone rang, and I glanced at the Caller I.D. *Restricted Call.* I had gotten this same type of call just yesterday, when Detective Smithy called. I had no doubt it was him again. I also had no doubt that it was going to be bad news.

"Hello, Detective," I said, answering, and waving for Ivy to keep quiet.

"Liz Turner was found dead in her jail cell an hour ago," he said without any preamble.

"Dead? How?"

"Bit off her tongue, bled to death in bed."

"But I thought she was on suicide watch."

"She was. And they thought she was asleep. By the time they suspected something was wrong... it was too late."

"Shit," I said.

"I second that," said the detective.

23.

The house, if anything, seemed even more ominous as it loomed before us.

And why wouldn't it? Now that I knew a demon had been roaming within it for nearly a century, I was, I would freely admit, scared shitless.

Ivy and I stood at the bottom of the driveway, holding hands. Ivy, for her part, stood with wide-eyed wonderment. Millicent warned me the girl was reckless. I would have to be wary of that. Or, at least, stay on the lookout for it... and maybe rein it in, if possible.

I was more than a little concerned Billy hadn't been answering my calls. Once I established a connection with someone, I could generally reconnect with them later. Unfortunately, I hadn't been able to re-establish the connection with Billy.

That, of course, concerned me even more.

In fact, I'd never *not* been able to re-establish a connection. What it meant was too horrible to consider.

I saw again the image I had seen days ago, when Billy had first appeared to me via the Psychic Hotline. It was an image I had been doing my best to ignore. So, I pushed it aside now... and walked up the driveway with Ivy by my side. We continued holding hands. There were no cars in the driveway this time.

As we approached the front door, the house seemed even bigger than I remembered. Perhaps knowing it was also the residence of something sick and sinister had changed my perception of its beauty. As we approached the darkened porch, I couldn't help but feel this was a very, very bad idea.

No, that wasn't it. This was a good idea. Ridding the Earth of this... *thing*... was a good idea. I knew, in fact, I was terrified to face it. I nearly turned around a half-dozen times and fled. In fact, it was Ivy's steady grip that propelled me further.

She and I were, of course, not alone.

There, standing at the front porch, drifting on the currents of space and time, was Millicent. I doubted Ivy could see her at the moment. It took a high level of second sight to see into the spirit world. I wasn't quite as adept at it as, say, Samantha Moon, but I was getting stronger, and my second sight was getting clearer. Millicent wasn't very clear. She was, in fact, an amorphous Millicent-shaped figure. By the way she stood, I knew her hands were clasped before her.

The plan had been simple. Millie would scout ahead, if possible. I knew she didn't have access to all places at all times. Some folks set boundaries around their home. Something as simple as, say, a saging of a house, or a blessing, or anything else designed to keep spirits away. Whether good or bad, all spirits were forced to recognize and respect such intentions.

"There are many lost souls within," she said. "But he is alone."

I nodded. "Good."

"But Allie..."

I knew what she would say. "I know," I said, taking in a lot of breath.

"You know what?" asked Ivy.

"I'm speaking with Millicent," I said.

"Oh, right. I wish I could do that someday."

I suspected she would, but for now, I looked at my spirit friend. "He's gone, isn't he?"

"Completely, child. He is lost to us."

I nodded. *Shit.*

"Who's gone?" asked Ivy.

I filled her in quickly and quietly. The street was silent. In fact, I heard no cars and saw no pedestrians. It was a perfect night for demon hunting.

"There's more, child," said Millicent. "There is death inside. Be prepared."

I nodded, although I wasn't sure how to prepare

myself. I warned Ivy as well. "Inside, there is death. Are you ready?"

There was, of course, a slightly wicked gleam in her eye. Yeah, she might be trouble. "As ready as I'll ever be."

I didn't bother knocking. Instead, I raised my hands, and, summoning the power always waiting within me—a power swirling in, around, and through me—I blew the front double doors off their hinges.

"Holy shit!" said Ivy when all the crashing finally subsided and the dust settled. "How did you —"

"Never mind that," I said, grabbing her hand. "C'mon."

24.

The stench was overwhelming.

I tried to fight the vomit that rose as I searched for a light switch. No good. As my groping hands hit a switch, I let go of Ivy's hand, turned my head and launched what I'd eaten for dinner tonight. I held myself up against the wall, as more of my dinner and probably some lunch and breakfast came up, too.

Ivy wasn't having the same problem. As I stood, wiping my mouth, she was already moving through the house.

"Wait—" I said, holding my stomach.

"It's coming from the kitchen. Stay here. Let me have a look. I have a feeling I can handle this stuff better than you. I played a crime scene investigator in my last movie and there was a lot of fake gore. You should have seen the gross things that I had to do..."

Mercifully, her voice trailed off as she turned through a door that I knew led to the kitchen. Never had I smelled something so fetid. So ripe, so dead, so overwhelming.

As Ivy stepped into the kitchen, she backed up quickly, stumbling, gasping, holding her hands to her face. She backed into the far wall. I think she even hit her head. Then she, too, turned and vomited.

Some heroes we are, I thought.

I had my phone in my hand before I realized it. My intent was to call the police. When you find a body, you call the police right? It seemed reasonable.

As I stood there in the entry hall, while Ivy, so brave, and yet, so foolish, vomited in the main hallway, I put my phone away. For now. Whoever was in there was dead. There was nothing we could do about that now. There was, however, still a chance we could remove the entity responsible for all of this.

I took some deep breaths through my mouth, tasting vomit—but at least I wasn't smelling the dead—I suddenly wished I had a gun, or that Samantha was with me. Or Smithy. Or Sanchez. Or the werewolf, Kingsley. Hell, I just wished I had a gun.

Ivy came back, wiping her mouth.

"Who was it?" I asked.

"I... I don't know. A woman. She's been dead for a few days, my guess. Bloated—"

I held up my hand, cutting her off. "Please."

"Calm yourself, child," said Millicent in my head, although I could not presently see her. "We have its attention. You will need to keep your wits about yourself. Go with Ivy and prepare the spell. I will distract it."

Be careful, I thought. But Millicent was already gone.

I paused briefly, took in a lot of air, and forced myself to stay calm. That a horrific demon was slithering through this house somewhere, I had no doubt. Millicent would do her part, but now, it was time to do ours.

I pushed away from the wall and, still breathing through my mouth, cleared the living room floor, tossing aside the coffee table and pulling away the rug. We needed an open space for the containment spell. Ivy, who had recovered from her shock, was by my side, helping.

"You okay?" I said to her.

She nodded and was about to speak, when a god-awful shriek shook the house to its very foundation. Ivy's eyes widened in terror. I had a feeling my expression matched hers.

I took her hands. "Are you ready?"

She nodded.

"Okay," I said. "You're on."

25.

Ivy got busy.

She removed a glass vial filled with powdered ingredients from an old, crusted pouch she had been carrying around her neck—it was an ancient leather satchel she found in an antique store and somehow, I knew it had been previously owned by another witch. And then, more vials and jars came out of the satchel, as if it was bottomless and huge, like the proverbial magic carpetbag. Ivy used the biggest vial like a mixing bowl.

I knew there were two schools of potioncraft: some witches followed spell recipes and got their ingredients decanted and mixed to a "T," and other witches trusted their inner knowing, mixing potion spells by instinct.

Ivy was the latter type of witch—no, she didn't use a spell book or any recipes. I watched her remove vials of wormwood and sulfur powder, jars of mandrake and kava kava. She added touches of this, dashes of that. Yes, she did seem to know what she was doing. But had she created an actual demonic binding potion?

Of that, I had no clue... and I could only pray Millicent and I had recruited the right witch.

Ivy sprinkled the ingredients in what appeared to be a semicircle. She pivoted in the center as she spread the mixture, which came out as a blue powder which was strange, since none of the raw ingredients were blue. She paused in the middle and looked at her handiwork, then corked the vial again. Once back in her pouch, she raised her hands, casting her gaze toward the ceiling—

And the lights in the house flickered... then went out completely, plunging us into complete darkness.

"Oh, shit," I said. Something bellowed... and scraped along the basement stairs. "It's coming!"

But Ivy wasn't paying attention to me. She was mumbling an incantation. She spoke faster and faster, repeating words and phrases, stringing them together in exactly the order they should go, instinctively knowing what to say.

Or so I hoped.

Badly hoped.

The floor shook as the demon clawed up the stairs, its nails screeching across wood like fingernails across a chalkboard. From behind me, something exploded and crashed across the kitchen floor. Probably the basement door.

In that moment, Millicent appeared before me. If a ghost could look out of breath, she did. Mostly, she looked alarmed. It was the first time I had seen anything but a serene expression on her face. Fighting demons tended to have that effect on witches, dead or alive.

"He's here, child," she said. "Is Ivy ready?"

As her answer, Ivy's mumbling turned into a shout and she raised her hands higher and turned in a circle—as she did so, the powdered ingredients erupted into blue flames.

And then, there was light.

I gasped and shielded my eyes.

Yes, it was only a semicircle. Ivy stepped out, breathless, and looked at me.

"Now you're on, Allie," she said.

26.

My heart hammering, I moved forward, standing before the flames, facing whatever it was that was coming out of the darkness.

I knew, of course, what it was. I had seen glimpses of it, but I had never come across something like this, face to face, and out in the open.

A demon.

Millicent was behind me, giving me support and strength. I felt her energy swim over me. Ivy was out of the burning semicircle, which flickered and roared behind me. She was behind me somewhere, too.

The house shook. The floor vibrated. The hallway walls, which glowed faintly from the blue firelight behind me, seemed to pulse. The Librarian had said the demon possessed the house itself. And the land. He said it could, quite literally, come from anywhere and everywhere at once.

"Oh, shit," said Ivy from behind me, and I could only imagine what she was thinking now. Surely, she regretted her decision in joining us. Or not. The girl was kind of nuts. Of course, that could be an asset right about now.

In the hallway before us, as the walls pulsed and the floor shook, a dark mass appeared, and I nearly peed myself.

"Be strong, child," came Millicent's words.

I could only fake a nod and hold my bladder, and wait for what I knew was coming.

I had my arms raised before me, before I even knew what I was doing. Truth was, I really didn't know what I was doing. Yes, I had mad psychic skills, but could I always trust them on a moment's notice? I didn't know. I hadn't used them that often.

Still, I felt the energy crackle around me. In particular, it came from around my hands. I could see what others couldn't: white flames surrounding my hands. No, they didn't burn my hands, and they weren't really flames. This was raw energy... and it was waiting for me to use it.

But was it of any use against a demon?

I didn't know, but Archibald Maximus had seemed to think so... and that was good enough for me. But what he couldn't predict was the fear that gripped me. Nor could he predict the unpredictable: the rage of a demon.

"Steady," said Millicent. But now, her words were only background noise.

The house creaked and shook and groaned. Windows even shattered. The entity truly seemed everywhere and anywhere.

Still, a darkness was forming in the hallway.

Filling the hallway.

Coming toward us.

I stepped back... and felt the heat of the ring of blue fire behind me.

"Easy, Allie," whispered Ivy.

From the hallway, which began across the living room, appeared a black mass, devoid of all light. The antithesis of light.

I heard myself say, "Oh, my God."

Ivy said something, too, but I missed it. Instead, I took another step back, and nearly singed my pants leg. Heat blasted me from behind, while a living shadow moved toward me from in front.

It poured out of the hallway slowly, billowing into the big living room. It could have been a dust cloud or fog, had either been blacker than black.

The fog coalesced, swirling slowly, and then faster and faster, until it took on the vague shape of a person. It stood, perhaps, eight feet tall.

This isn't happening, I thought. No way is this happening.

"Easy, child." Millicent was my rock right now.

Two red eyes opened in the region of the head. They focused on me, and now I couldn't be entirely sure that I didn't pee myself.

"Oh, fuck," said Ivy behind me, pretty much echoing my thoughts.

Horrific images flooded my mind. I saw death and blood and corpses. I saw torture and fire and rotting flesh. I saw scurrying rats and snakes and the fearsome eyes of an enraged demon.

The images I knew, were from *It*.

As the shadow regarded me, I heard slow footsteps, then the sound of clapping. The clapping and footsteps echoed down through the hallway, and they somehow seemed more amplified than they should have been.

As the footsteps drew closer, and the clapping resounded seemingly everywhere at once, a human figure stepped through the tall shadow, which dissipated in a puff of wispy black smoke.

The figure was, of course, the Englishman.

Billy Turner.

He continued clapping as he stepped deeper into the big living room, his features awash in blue light. "Now, *that* was a smashing entrance, was it not?"

But, of course, it sounded nothing like Billy. Gone was the English accent, replaced by something harsh and guttural and filled with mock humor.

"Billy," I said, but I knew it was a waste to address him by his human name. There was no human expression on that contorted, stretched face. His eyes were too wide. The smile was too big. Nostrils were too flared. Eyebrows were too high. It was as if Billy Turner had been caught doing exactly what all of our mothers had warned us against: making funny faces and having them stay that way.

His eyes, I noted, didn't move in their sockets. At least, I didn't think they did. As he took in both me and Ivy, he turned his head slowly from side to side, rather than shifting his eyes. It was all... so... damn... weird.

He was totally and completely possessed. Of that, I was sure. Billy Turner the Englishman, the human, was long gone, and that saddened me greatly.

Billy lifted his head. "Aw, I sense great fear and sadness. Music to my ears, so to speak." He stepped deeper into the big room, and scanned the furniture that had been pushed aside, then his head swiveled, taking in the blue ring of fire.

"It looks like to me that there's some kind of ceremony going on." He sniffed the air. "I smell vervain and mugwort. Nasty stuff." He turned his wide-eyed gaze back on me. So far, I was certain he had not blinked. "If I didn't know better, I would think you were trying to get rid of me. Now, that's not very nice."

I finally found my voice. "Leave the house, Billy. This is between the demon and us."

Billy, with his raised eyebrows and wrinkled forehead, regarded me for a moment, as black, wispy snakes continued coiling around him. Around and around and through him. "Yes, I can see that I will have to deal with you, in much the same way that I dealt with my nosy neighbor. She's behind me in the kitchen, rotting and putrefying. In fact..." He paused and sniffed the air. "I can smell her now. My favorite aroma, if you will. Death and rot."

"You're a fucking piece of shit," said Ivy suddenly, stepping forward. "I'm going to enjoy watching you rot in hell."

Billy glanced at Ivy. "This one has spirit, I see. She will make a fine plaything. But first—" Billy reached behind him and removed a knife that might have been stained with blood, although the flickering blue flames didn't quite give off enough light to know for certain. "First, I have to destroy *this* plaything."

Billy brought the knife up to his own throat.

And slit it straight across.

27.

I screamed as Billy's head flopped forward, and he dropped to his knees.

I rushed forward, but a blast of cold wind, followed by a swirling shadow, literally threw me backward. I tumbled head over ass and ended up in a heap along the far wall. I looked up from the floor in time to see the once-frozen expression on Billy's face replaced by one of shocked horror. A human expression. Billy reached up to his damaged neck, then pitched forward, choking and gagging, and then lay still.

"Oh, fuck!" screamed Ivy. "Oh, fuck."

I found my feet and located the swirling mass which hovered briefly over Billy. It seemed to be gathering itself, solidifying. The red eyes returned, and looked directly at me.

It charged.

***

Ivy screamed.

I raised my hands as a wall of white light appeared around me, the exact energy I had been instructed by the Librarian to use. The wall surrounded me completely... except that the demon altered its course... and disappeared down between cracks in the floorboards.

"Where did it go?" I shouted, rushing forward to where it had disappeared. The floor shook... and seemed to expand up and out, like a breathing thing.

"Behind you!" shouted Millie in my head.

I spun around to discover the demon pouring out of the floorboards, drifting up the many horizontal slots, like black smoke through a vent.

It came up from directly beneath Ivy, lifting her.

I ran toward her, leaping over the flames, covering my face as the heat blasted me. But she was already pressed up against the high, vaulted ceiling. The swirling darkness beneath her—the utter blackness that held her up—was without shape. However, I suspected what it would do next... and I was right.

It promptly disappeared and Ivy began falling.

I didn't try to catch her. She was too high; hell, she would have broken my back. Instead, I did the only thing I could think of: I raised both hands with the intention to psychically cushion her fall. And that mostly worked. Halfway through her drop, Ivy hit whatever force I was generally exuding, rebounded off it, paused briefly in mid-air and then crashed to the floor.

I was at her side, but she waved me away. "I'm fine. Just—look out!"

Without turning, I raised my hands again and released whatever was left in me. It seemed to be enough. Still holding my hands up, I turned and saw that I had captured myself a demon.

There it was, contained within a vortex of energy that both my hands were creating. How I created this, I didn't know. From where the power came, I could only guess: Mother Earth herself. Either way, I was using it, and the demon seemed bound within.

The darkness and light intermixed and it was truly something to behold. Light and dark, side by side, fighting, battling.

The demon, at present, was still in its smoke state, but as the energy continued to swirl around it, it took on more shape. Shortly, as I stepped around it, holding my hands up, it turned into something bigger than it had been before. Great horns curved up from its black head. The eyes were redder, angrier, and filled with so much hate I wanted to run from this place, screaming.

But I didn't. The white light also kept it out of my mind: no more images of fear and death and evil.

At present, it was behind me, contained within

my energy, and I knew just what to do. And Ivy knew what to do, too, even though it was obvious she was seriously injured from her fall.

My new friend, and the newest member of the witch triad, crawled on her hands and knees. As she did so, I guided the demon over the floor, keeping my hands up, as it swirled and formed and reformed, eyes flashing red, and swept him into the semicircle.

But it wasn't a semicircle for long.

Ivy used the rest of the blue powder to seal off the circle. Immediately, the blue flame caught on and formed a full circle that completely surrounded the demon. I lowered my arms, and it dropped down within the ring of fire.

And screeched hideously.

I stumbled back, gasping, as Millicent made a full appearance, looking so solid that she might as well have been alive again. She raised her hands, and began uttering a complicated spell.

With each word, the demon writhed more and more, and still she continued the incantation. She stepped closer and closer, and the demon shrieked louder and louder.

Ivy stared up from the floor. Her leg was at an awkward angle. But she had come through. The blue fire illuminated her pretty face... and seemed to go right through Millicent.

The demon grew in size and fought the wall of blue fire, pounding it with clawed fists.

I couldn't believe I was here, seeing this now, a

part of something so... out of this world. But here I was, gasping, feeling the heat from the fire, and watching a ghost witch finish off the demon.

And finish it off, Millicent did.

A moment later, the floor beneath the demon seemed to open up. I sensed a great hole beneath it, although I couldn't see it. The demon dropped, plummeting down... and was gone.

Mother Earth was waiting. What she would do with the entity, I didn't know, but she had promised it would be gone, forever.

And I always believed Mother.

28.

Later that night, I was sitting with Smithy in his squad car.

Ivy had already been taken to the local hospital, where she was being treated for a broken ankle. That she had crawled across the floor with a broken ankle... to seal the ring of fire... was still mind-blowing to me. Yeah, she had my respect.

"And the demon is really gone?" he asked. I had just gotten the ill-kempt detective up to date.

"Yes," I said.

"Did I just say 'demon'?" Smithy asked.

"You did, Detective. Welcome to my world."

"I'm not sure I like your world," he said.

I shrugged. "The two are tied together. The demon had been orchestrating a series of deaths for many, many decades. You could probably single-handedly close some of these cold cases related to deaths in this house—"

"No, I can't, because no one would believe me."

"But you believe me," I said.

"I'm not sure I do."

"You do. You just won't admit it. It scares you to admit it."

"I ain't afraid of shit," he said. "Well, maybe a red-eyed demon."

We were quiet. Outside, the crime scene guys weren't quiet. They came and went inside the big home. Earlier, I had watched as they'd wheeled out a gurney covered by a big sheet. The sheet was bigger than Billy had been. I knew, of course, that he had been dead for days... and had bloated, as corpses were wont to do. The Billy that I had seen inside the house, slitting his own throat... that Billy had become the demon's puppet at that point. I had likely never seen the real Billy, aside from his initial phone call to the Psychic Hotline.

Smithy stepped out of the car and spoke to his crew, only to come back and report that the corpse was, indeed, probably Billy Turner. However, it was still hard to verify that yet, since the body was in such poor condition. He did confirm that Billy's neck wound appeared to be self-inflicted. However, it was still too early to tell for sure. And the female corpse in the kitchen was a missing neighbor whose frantic family had filed a report only two days before.

"How... how could a demon do that?" asked Smithy. "I mean, they don't have bodies, right?"

"No, but they operate out of fear and, in fact, they feed on it. It didn't need hands if humans were willing to kill for it."

"But... why would they kill for it?"

"I suspect this demon worked slowly at first, meaning, it first came into their lives through their dreams. From there, it preyed on fear and depression and drugs—and anything else that would give it an 'in.'"

"Did they know the demon was there? I mean, were they aware of it?"

"Maybe," I said. "But I doubt it. Unable to resist it, each of the homeowners undoubtedly found themselves in a darker and darker space, until they, too, could be fully possessed."

"Jesus! So, what can people do against a demon? How would they resist something like this? Not everyone is, you know, a witch."

"Fortify your home with blessings. Sage your home—"

"Sage it?" he interrupted.

"The herb, sage, is known to repel negative energy and malicious spirits. And you should be aware immediately if, say, you feel unreasonably depressed or sad or angry."

"But some people do get sad and depressed and angry."

"But not unreasonably so, and not without good reason. Often such feelings are followed by disturbing thoughts."

"And this is the demon causing those thoughts?" Smithy asked.

"Perhaps, perhaps not."

"What would someone do next?"

"Meditate and pray, and perhaps bring in a holy man or woman. Someone to further bless yourself and your home. The key is to not let anything get out of hand. Demons and other, darker entities must, in the end, obey the light."

"Did you say darker entities? Lord help me."

"That's a good prayer, too," I said, and nudged him in the gut.

"And you really, you know, defeated the demon... using your, you know, magic?"

He comically waved his hands in front of him.

I giggled. It was a much-needed giggle.

"I had help," I said.

"So, is it really gone? Is it really over?" he asked.

"I think so, yes."

"But there are other demons out there, right?"

"I imagine so."

"God, I hope I never cross paths with something like that."

"And if you do..."

"Right, you'd better believe I'm calling you."

"Why, detective, I'm flattered."

He grumbled, then looked at me long and hard. There was a chance—a small chance—that he might have trimmed his mustache straight this time.

And then, he smiled and it went all haywire again.

"I'm glad you're okay, kiddo," he said.

"So am I."

"We're going to have to be creative with your witness statement."

"We'll think of something," I said. "Can you take my statement tomorrow?"

He nodded. "Good idea. You can drive yourself home in just a few minutes. It looks like the forensics team is releasing your car without tearing it apart."

"There's nothing in it that relates to what happened here."

"Nope. There isn't. Excuse me for a minute." He gave me a half smile and stepped out of the car.

Millie the ghost appeared in the driver's seat that had just been occupied by the detective.

"You did good today," she said.

"So did you," I said aloud, although quietly. No one outside of the car would have heard me.

"Are you okay?" she asked.

"I liked him."

"The Englishman?"

"Yes," I said.

"He's free now."

"He's also dead. No offense."

She nodded and didn't seem offended, then reached out and took my hand. I mostly didn't feel it, except for a small, warm tingle. I did my best to squeeze back, as we sat there together, watching the crime scene investigators pour in and out of the big, dark, demon-free home.

My phone whistled, startling me. A text message. I considered ignoring it, but instead, reached into my jeans pocket and pulled out my Galaxy Note.

It was a message from Samantha Moon. *You've been quiet.*

I've been fighting a demon, I texted back.

Did you win?

Of course.

Glad to hear it. Drinks tonight?

I thought you would never ask.

The kids are with Mary Lou. I'll be there in an hour.

Drinks with a vampire after vanquishing a demon and sitting next to a ghost.

Yeah, my life is weird, but I wouldn't have it any other way.

The End

About the Author:

J.R. Rain is an ex-private investigator who now writes full-time. He lives in a small house on a small island with his small dog, Sadie. Please visit him at www.jrrain.com.

Made in the USA
Middletown, DE
28 December 2022

20578930R00096